喚醒你的英文語感！

Get a Feel for English !

喚醒你的英文語感！

Get a Feel for English !

最有力量的英文
藝術天才經典名言

Great Quotes
from
Great Artists

作　者 ◎ David Katz、王復國

IRT 語言測驗中心
Language Testing Center

貝塔語言出版
Beta Multimedia Publishing

Contents

本書使用說明

本書收錄了從古至今共 140 位最具影響力的藝術家之經典名言，共 212 句，分別歸類在 Success（成功）、Dreams（夢想）、Creativity（創意）、Action（行動）、Work（工作）等十五個主題之下。

● 「**Close-up 焦點人物**」：詳細介紹了該章代表大師之背景、畫派、特色及歷史定位，中英文對照呈現，生難字詞並輔以註解。

● 其他大師名言：附上該位藝術大師的簡歷，概略的名言背景介紹，以及生難字詞或特殊用語解析。

Track 02 利用 MP3 感受撼動人心的名言

MP3 中收錄了本書所有英語名言及藝術家人名。
請各位用耳朵來享受藝術天才們的名言饗宴。

Success
成功

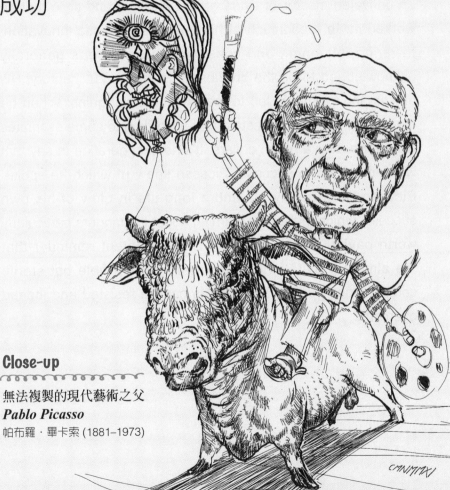

無法複製的現代藝術之父
Pablo Picasso
帕布羅．畢卡索 (1881–1973)

From painting to sculpture, from his early realist works to his cubist masterpieces and beyond, Pablo Picasso was an unrivaled master of every artistic medium and style that he worked in. In recognition of his relentless stylistic innovation, towering influence, and consummate skill, he is generally acknowledged to be the greatest artist of the 20th century. His artistic achievements led to massive financial gains. When he died in 1973, he left an estate that according to some estimates was worth over a billion dollars. It's no exaggeration to say that when it comes to success, Picasso knew of which he spoke. Picasso lived nearly his entire long life in glow of his own success, which makes his warning about its dangers particularly worth paying attention to. His art is a potent reminder that the almost gravitational pull toward comfortable but sterile complacency that success exerts can be resisted and indeed overcome.

從繪畫到雕塑，從早期的現實主義作品到他的立體派傑作等等，在他所投入的各種藝術媒介和風格中，帕布羅‧畢卡索都是無與倫比的大師。有鑑於他持續不懈的風格創新、歷久不衰的影響力，以及登峰造極的技巧，他被公認為 20 世紀最偉大的藝術家。他的藝術成就更帶來了豐厚的金錢收入。據估計，在他 1973 年去世時所留下的遺產總值超過了 10 億美元。說畢卡索最清楚什麼叫成功一點也不為過。畢卡索漫長的一生幾乎都活在自己的成功光環中，因此他對於成功的危險所提出的警告特別值得留意。他的藝術深切提醒了大家，成功會使人幾乎一面倒地耽溺於安逸卻貧乏的自滿中，然而人可以抗拒並確實克服這點。

Notes

cubist [ˈkjubɪst] *adj.* 立體派主義的
unrivaled [ʌnˈraɪvld] *adj.* 無敵的
relentless [rɪˈlɛntlɪs] *adj.* 不懈的
consummate [ˈkɑnsəmet] *adj.* 技藝高超的
exaggeration [ɪɡˌzædʒəˈreʃən] *n.* 誇大
potent [ˈpotn̩t] *adj.* 強有力的
gravitational [ɡrævəˈteʃən̩l] *adj.* 重力的
sterile [ˈstɛrəl] *adj.* 貧瘠的
complacency [kəmˈplesn̩sɪ] *n.* 自滿
exert [ɪɡˈzɝt] *v.* 發揮

> *Success is dangerous. One begins to copy oneself, and to copy oneself is more dangerous than to copy others. It leads to sterility.*

Pablo Picasso

「成功是危險的。人會開始模仿自己,而模仿自己比模仿他人更危險。如此會導致貧乏。」

Notes

sterility [ˈstɛrələtɪ] *n.* 貧乏

英文用法解析

注意，在比較結構中用來比較的兩個項目須平行對等，如本例中 to copy oneself 和 to copy others 皆為不定詞片語。若改為 copying oneself is more dangerous than copying others 亦合乎文法。

本章的名言分為兩大類，第一類談的是要如何邁向成功。畢卡索和萊特 (Wright) 十分強調傳統的途徑：規劃、目標、努力、逐步改善。米開朗基羅 (Michelangelo) 提醒我們，要偉大就必須以「偉大」而非以「足夠」為目標。歐姬芙 (O'Keeffe) 和奧德特 (Audette) 則提出了較發人深省的觀點。第二類名言的重點則在於如何評估一件藝術作品或一個藝術家之成功與否。塞尚 (Cézanne)、夏卡爾 (Chagall) 和伍德林 (Woodring) 指出，成功的作品必須包含一些靈感元素。奧斯頓 (Allston)、羅斯 (Ross) 和肯特 (Kent) 則認為一個成功的藝術家要能內省，而不須靠任何外在的確認。對達利 (Dali)（那個無賴！）來說，能激起別人的嫉妒而以此為樂就是成功。

Success 2

Our goals can only be reached through a vehicle of a plan, in which we must fervently believe, and upon which we must vigorously act. There is no other route to success.

「我們的目標只能透過計畫來達成,我們必須對該計畫深信不疑,而且必須全力以赴。成功沒有別條路可走。」

Pablo Picasso 帕布羅・畢卡索 (1881–1973) ⇨P. 1
西班牙藝術家,以源源不絕的創造力開啓了立體派繪畫,並樹立現代藝術的實驗精神。

據估計,畢卡索創作了 5 萬件橫跨各種媒介與風格的藝術作品。此外還有兩任妻子、無數個情婦,以及傳說中的社交行程表。顯然這個男人很清楚要怎麼把事情做好。

Success 3

I know the price of success: dedication, hard work and an unremitting devotion to the things you want to see happen.

「我知道成功的代價:投入、努力,以及持續不斷為想要做到的事付出。」

Frank Lloyd Wright 法蘭克·洛依德·萊特 (1867–1959)
美國建築師、室內設計師、作家與教育家，提倡有機式建築。

「成功的代價」可以有兩個意思。萊特在這裡的意思是「獲致成功的必要條件」。而「成功的代價」更常用來指邁向成功後往往會失去的東西，像是隱私、友情和動力等。

Success 4

The greater danger for most of us lies not in setting our aim too high and falling short; but in setting our aim too low, and achieving our mark.

「對大多數人來說，較大的危險不在於把目標訂得太高並以失敗收場，而在於把目標訂得太低並順利達到。」

Michelangelo 米開朗基羅 (1475–1564) ⇨P. 43
文藝復興三傑之一，尤以雕塑奇才著稱，代表作為西斯汀教堂壁畫。

米開朗基羅認為，成功的意義不應只是「達成目標」，尤其是如果目標太過平庸。米開朗基羅為自己樹立的高標準極具傳奇性。有則著名的故事說，他曾用錘子把摩西雕像的膝蓋給敲碎，並大喊道：「跟我說話啊！」

Notes

fervently [ˈfɝvəntlɪ] *adv.* 熱烈地；強烈的
vigorously [ˈvɪgərəslɪ] *adv.* 精力旺盛地
route [rut] *n.* 路；路線

unremitting [ˌʌnrɪˈmɪtɪŋ] *adj.* 從不間斷的
fall short (of) 未達……；不及……

You get whatever accomplishment you are willing to declare.

「只要願意說出口，一切的成就就是你的。」

Georgia O'Keeffe 喬琪亞・歐姬芙 (1887–1986)
美國現代女畫家代表，以描繪大自然花卉草葉及沙漠中的骨骸聞名於世。

這句話與俗話 "You get what you deserve." 「你該得到什麼就會得到什麼。」呈現出有趣的對比。身為在由男人主導的藝術界中成功的女性畫家，歐姬芙可能無意嘲諷，或許她只是針對才華與成功之間經常出現的極大落差做出她的評論。

Yes, we can all be huge fucking winners; if we just put our minds to it. And, possess a whole shit-load of luck, and are willing to mercilessly and ruthlessly crush someone to do it. But, they never tell you that last part. That part is ugly.

「沒錯，我們全都能成為他媽的大贏家，只要我們有心這麼做，而且又有狗屎運，並願意無情又殘忍地踩在別人頭上來達到目的。但是他們從來不把最後一部分告訴你。那部分很醜陋。」

Derek R. Audette 德瑞克‧奧德特 (1971–)
加拿大 X 世代藝術家，創作橫跨抽象畫作、數位藝術、音樂、詩作。

奧德特是一位年輕的當代藝術家，他歸納了幾個在大師的成功法則裡所看不到的因素：運氣和無情。這是我們這個時代的縮影，或者只是個別藝術家的獨門見解，就留給讀者去評斷了。

👍 Measuring Success 評估成功

Success 7

When I judge art, I take my painting and put it next to a God-made object like a tree or flower. If it clashes, it is not art.

「我在評斷藝術時，會把我的畫放在造物主的作品旁邊，比如像一棵樹或一朵花。假如兩相不搭，它就不是藝術。」

Paul Cézanne 保羅‧塞尚 (1839–1906) ⇨P. 75
法國印象派大師，以光影色彩實踐量體與空間的現代繪畫之父。

God-made 指「上帝創造的」，是 man-made「人造的」之相對詞。類似結構的字還有 home-made「家裡做的」、machine-made「機器製造的」、self-made「自製的」、tailor-made「訂製的」等。

Notes

mercilessly [ˋmɝsɪlɪslɪ] *adv.* 無情地
ruthlessly [ˋruθlɪslɪ] *adv.* 殘酷地

When I am finishing a picture, I hold some God-made object up to it—a rock, a flower, the branch of a tree or my hand—as a final test. If the painting stands up beside a thing man cannot make, the painting is authentic. If there's a clash between the two, it's bad art.

「當我快要完成一幅畫時，我會拿一樣造物主的作品擺到它旁邊，比如一顆石頭、一朵花、一根樹枝或是我的手，來作為最後的測試。假如在人做不出來的東西旁邊，畫能挺立，這就是一幅真的好畫。假如兩者不搭的話，那就是差勁的藝術。」

Marc Chagall 馬克‧夏卡爾 (1887–1985)
二十世紀最偉大的猶太籍畫家，擅用色彩表現情感，風格介於後印象與野獸派之間，超現實主義者奉他為先驅。

───────────────────────────

夏卡爾很欣賞塞尚，所以當然有可能聽過塞尚的名言，但我寧可認為，這兩位偉大的藝術家是各自得到相同的結論。

Every time I write something down I check it to see if it has that telltale glow, the glow that tells me there's something there. If it glows, it stays. Everything is either on or off.

「每當我寫了什麼東西時，我都會檢查一下，看看它有沒有那種掩蓋不住的光芒，也就是那種能告訴我那裡有某樣東西的光芒。假如發光了，它就能留下來。每樣東西不是發光就是不發光。」

Jim Woodring 吉姆‧伍德林 (1952–)
美國卡通、漫畫家與玩具設計師，作品以超現實風格為主。

伍德林是偉大的漫畫家，信奉印度的宗教哲學吠檀多。他跟塞尚及夏卡爾一樣，是以有沒有靈感元素——「那種掩蓋不住的光芒」——來衡量成功與否。

Success 10

The only competition worthy of a wise man is with himself.

「對一個聰明的人而言，唯一值得競爭的就是自己。」

Washington Allston 華盛頓‧奧斯頓 (1779–1843)
美國畫家與詩人，美國風景畫之先導，擅長畫古典風景和聖經故事。

奧斯頓是美國的浪漫派畫家，讀過哈佛和倫敦皇家學院，過著紳士的生活。他的崇拜者當中不乏同時代的頂尖藝術家和詩人，但此處所表達的想法一點都不假。在人生接近尾聲之際，他婉拒了所有的委託，為的是創作一幅非比尋常的巨大繪畫，而且這將成為他的傑作。可惜在完成以前，他就過世了。

Notes

authentic [ɔˋθɛntɪk] *adj.* 真實的；可靠的
telltale [ˋtɛl͵tel] *adj.* 洩漏秘密的；遮掩不了的（證據等）

Traditionally, art has been for the select few. We have been brainwashed to believe that Michelangelo had to pat you on the head at birth. Well, we show people that anybody can paint a picture that they're proud of. It may never hang in the Smithsonian, but it will certainly be something that they'll hang in their home and be proud of. And that's what it's all about.

「傳統上，藝術一直是菁英分子的玩意兒。我們都被洗腦而相信，米開朗基羅必須在你出生時拍拍你的頭。嗯，我們要告訴大家的是，任何人都能畫出讓自己引以為傲的畫。它也許永遠不會被掛在史密森尼博物館裡，但是肯定可以掛在自己家裡並引以為傲。藝術就是這麼一回事。」

Bob Ross 包伯‧羅斯 (1942–1995)
美國家喻戶曉的繪畫教學節目「樂在畫畫」(*The Joy of Painting*) 主持人與畫作指導者。

「樂在畫畫」播出長達 12 年，羅斯教導了無數的美國人如何畫畫，並且和千百萬觀眾分享了如何欣賞藝術與人生。他十足的親和力和持續不斷的鼓勵，與眾家大師主張的刻苦奉獻形成了強烈的對比。

Life is a succession of moments, to live each one is to succeed.

「人生是一連串的時刻，過好每一刻就是成功。」

Corita Kent 柯莉塔‧肯特 (1918–1986)
美國知名絹版畫家，為美國聖母無玷大學修女與藝術導師。

一般人在提到極具創意的普普藝術家時，通常不會聯想到「修女」，而柯莉塔‧肯特就是一位修女。她首開先河把平面設計與主張和平與社會正義的訊息結合起來，因而拉近了藝術與生活之間的距離。

The thermometer of success is merely the jealousy of the malcontents.

「成功的溫度計不過就是不平者的嫉妒罷了。」

Salvador Dali 薩爾瓦多‧達利
西班牙超現實主義畫家，以奇想象徵物的營造探討人的夢境與慾望。

恰好與奧斯頓形成對比，達利完全把成功定位在自身以外。假如有人愛他，他就是被愛了。假如有人恨他，那他就成功了！

Notes

succession [sək`sɛʃən] *n.* 一連串；一系列
thermometer [θə`mɑmətə] *n.* 一連串；一系列
malcontent [`mælkən,tɛnt] *n.* 不滿現狀的人

Chapter 2

Dreams
夢想

Close-up

達達與超現實藝術的奠基者
Man Ray
曼恩·雷 (1890–1976)

MAN RAY

Man Ray sometimes claimed that he didn't record his dreams, but of course that's exactly what he did. He had a narrow shelf that could be swung out over his bed, and as soon as he woke up, he would sketch his dreams on it, sketches that would often be developed into finished artworks. This was not an unusual practice among surrealist artists like Ray, who, in the words of André Breton's *Surrealist Manifesto*, recognized the "omnipotence of dream." But Man Ray's life also exemplified the other kind of dream: dream as aspiration. In many ways, Man Ray lived the life of his dreams—the life of the archetypal artist. After successful showings of his paintings, photographs, and assemblages in his native New York, he turned up in Paris in 1921 where he was warmly received by the most influential artists and writers of the generation—Picasso and Dali, Hemmingway and Joyce. In the years that followed, when he wasn't cavorting with famous French singers or inventing new photography techniques, he shot models for leading fashion magazines and was influential in the development of both Dada and Surrealism. Not bad for the son of an immigrant Jewish tailor in New York who (to his parents' dismay) turned down a scholarship to study architecture in order to follow his dream of becoming an artist.

曼恩‧雷有時候宣稱他並沒有把他的夢記錄下來，而事實上他做的就是把夢給記錄下來。他的床邊有一個架子可以隨時轉到床的上方，這樣他一醒來就能在上面把夢畫下來，而且這些畫經常會發展成完整的藝術作品。對於像雷這種超現實主義畫家來說，這麼做並不稀奇。一如安德烈‧布雷頓在《超現實主義宣言》中所說的，「夢無所不能」，但是曼恩‧雷的人生也印證了另一種夢：胸懷大志的夢。在許多方面，曼恩‧雷都實現了他的夢想人生，也就是典型藝術家的人生。在家鄉紐約成功展出他的繪畫、攝影和集合藝術作品之後，曼恩‧雷在 1921 年時來到巴黎，受到了當代重量級藝術家與作家熱烈歡迎，包括畢卡索和達利，海明威和喬伊斯。在接下來的幾年中，當他沒有跟法國的知名歌星廝混或發明新的攝影技術的時候，他就幫頂尖時尚雜誌拍攝模特兒。達達主義和超現實主義的發展也都受到他的影響。身為猶太移民與紐約裁縫師之子，他表現得相當出色，他甚至為了實現當藝術家的夢想，而放棄了攻讀建築的獎學金，這一點則令他的父母頗為失望。

Notes

surrealist [sə`riəlɪst] *n.* 超現實主義者
omnipotence [ɑm`nɪpətn̩s] *n.* 全能
archetypal [`ɑrkɪ͵taɪpl] *adj.* 原型的
assemblage [ə`sɛmblɪdʒ] *n.* 集合在一起的人或物
cavort [kə`vɔrt] *v.* （人）歡鬧

Dream 1

> ***It has never been my object to record my dreams, just the determination to realize them.***

Man Ray

「我的目的從來不是把夢記錄下來，而是決心實現它們。」

英文用法解析

曼恩‧雷曾說：「我拍的不是自然，而是我的想像。」但是曼恩‧雷不只是個超現實主義者，他出道時是個商業藝術家兼插畫家，在他大紅大紫後，他依舊為《時尚》、《哈潑時尚》和其他雜誌從事攝影工作，以藉此支付開銷。

要找到不重視夢想和作夢的藝術家，幾乎不可能，而要找對於價值的看法一致的藝術家，幾乎同樣困難。M.C. 艾薛爾跟曼恩‧雷一樣，認為夢想世界的藝術體現能揭露另一個也就是我們所居住的世界的真相。大衛‧霍克尼 (David Hockney) 和威廉‧艾倫 (William Allan) 聲稱，藝術家必須實現個人的夢想。威廉‧莫里斯 (William Morris) 和小野洋子 (Yoko Ono) 則認為夢想是重要的集體活動。對於馬克‧夏卡爾、文森‧梵谷、李奧納多‧達文西、尼奧‧勞奇 (Neo Rauch)、喬吉奧‧德‧基里科 (Giorgio de Chirico) 以及法蘭茲‧馬克 (Franz Marc) 等諸多藝術家而言，夢想是藝術的基本素材，在他們看來，藝術是通往夢想世界的入口。芙烈達‧卡洛 (Frieda Khalo) 和古斯塔夫‧莫羅 (Gustave Moreau) 把這層關係拉得更近，他們兩人都認為，最重要的就是現實本身如夢一般的本質。

Only those who attempt the absurd will achieve the impossible. I think it's in my basement ... let me go upstairs and check.

「只有願意嘗試荒謬的人才能成就不可能的事。我想它就在我的地下室裡……我上樓去看看。」

M. C. Escher M. C. 艾薛爾 (1898–1972)
荷蘭現代藝術家，擅於創造複雜的結構與混淆視覺的圖案，靈感取自阿拉伯的幾何圖騰。

水看起來是往上流向瀑布、男子隨意地坐在天花板上、人群下了樓梯卻沒往下走──艾薛爾扭曲現實的畫作涵蓋了這一切的不可能。

Dreams as Aspiration 胸懷大志的夢

The mind is the limit. As long as the mind can envision the fact that you can do something, you can do it, as long as you really believe 100 percent.

「腦袋是極限之所在。只要腦袋有辦法想像你做得到某件事，你就做得到，只要你能百分之百相信。」

David Hockney 大衛・霍克尼 (1937–)

英國現代藝術家，擅以畫作猶如攝影鏡頭般地捕捉陽光下的動靜。

As long as 或 so long as 為片語連接詞，用來引導表「範圍、條件」之副詞子句，意思是「只要」。其所引導的子句可置於句首（如本例）或句尾，如：You can stay here as long as you keep quiet.「只要你保持安靜，就可以待在這裡。」

Dream 4

Father, in spite of all this spending of money in learning Latin, I will be a painter.

「爸，儘管學拉丁文花了這麼多錢，我還是要當畫家。」

William Allan 威廉・亞倫 (1782–1850)

蘇格蘭皇家學院院長與畫家，以俄國的歷史與風景畫著稱。

In spite of 為片語介系詞，相當於介系詞 despite，一般用來表達「讓步」，意思是「儘管」。在 in spite of 或 despite 之後必須使用名詞結構，如本句中的名詞片語 all this spending of money in learning Latin。

Notes

absurb [əb`sɜd] *adj.* 荒謬的
envision [ɪn`vɪʒən] *v.* 想像

If others can see it as I have seen it, then it may be called a vision rather than a dream.

「假如別人與我所見略同，那它或許可以叫做理想，而不是夢想。」

William Morris 威廉・莫里斯 (1834–1896)
英國工藝美術運動發起人，為反對工業設計標準化而成立自己的設計公司。

Vision 這個字可用來指「視力、視覺」、「幻想、幻影」。但是在本句中指的是一種「對未來的構想」或「理想」，甚至「遠見」。例如我們可以說：Bill Gates is a man of vision.「比爾・蓋茲是個有遠見的人。」

A dream you dream alone is only a dream. A dream you dream together is reality.

「你自己一個作的夢只是個夢。大家一起作的夢就會成真。」

Yoko Ono 小野洋子 (1933–)
日裔美籍前衛藝術家，約翰藍儂之妻，同時也是音樂家與和平運動支持者。

這是小野在多年前所寫的話，收錄於由約翰・藍儂、小野洋子和大衛・薛夫合著之《我們所說的話：約翰・藍儂與小野洋子的最後主要訪談》(*All We Are Saying: The Last Major Interview with John Lennon and Yoko Ono*)。

I sometimes have the impression that I have been born between heaven and earth … the more I work the more I tried to align these paintings with a distant dream.

「我生於天地之間的印象有時候會浮現在我的腦海中……我畫得愈多，就愈想要把這些畫跟遙遠的夢想串連起來。」

Marc Chagall 馬克‧夏卡爾

夏卡爾的出生地是當時俄羅斯帝國中一個以猶太人為主的城鎮，叫做維鐵斯克。夏卡爾所說遙遠的夢想就是他年輕時在那裡的夢想。他的作品有很多是在回憶當年猶太村落的生活，而這樣的生活在一次世界大戰期間受到重創，後來更在二次世界大戰中被納粹消滅殆盡。

N o t e s

align [ə`laɪn] *v.* 排成一列

Why does the eye see a thing more clearly in dreams than with the imagination being awake?

「在夢中所見的東西為什麼會比清醒時的想像還清楚？」

Leonardo da Vinci 李奧納多・達文西 (1452–1519)
義大利文藝復興三傑之最長者，精通科學人文與人體解剖的全人藝術大師。

本句使用了比較結構，而比較結構中被比較的兩個項目必須平行對等，例如在本句被拿來比較的 in dreams 和 with the imagination being awake，兩者都是介系詞片語。

For me, painting means the continuation of dreaming by other means.

「對我來說，畫畫就是不斷靠其他的方法來作夢。」

Neo Rauch 尼奧・勞奇 (1960–)
德國畫家，創作融合了美國漫畫美學式的場景與共產主義的社會現實主義。

尼奧・勞奇出生於東德的萊比錫，雖然他對於是否該把自己歸類為超寫實畫家有所遲疑，但是他的作品常給人一種如謎般的夢幻感覺。

N o t e s

means [minz] *n.* 手段；方法

I dream of painting and then I paint my dream.

「我夢想著畫畫，然後把我的夢畫出來。」

Vincent van Gogh　文森・梵谷 (1853–1890) ⇨P. 59
荷蘭後印象派畫家，以短暫的生命熱情擁抱藝術，如烈日下燃燒的靈魂。

梵谷是當今市場上最搶手、作品最昂貴的畫家之一。一生痛苦潦倒，發瘋甚至自殺身亡的梵谷（死時年僅 37 歲）若地下有知，不知對此作何感想。

To become truly immortal, a work of art must escape all human limits: logic and common sense will only interfere. But once these barriers are broken, it will enter the realms of childhood visions and dreams.

「如果一件藝術作品要永垂不朽，它就必須擺脫一切人為的侷限：邏輯和常識只會壞事。然而一旦把這些障礙給打破，它就會進入童年夢幻與夢想的領域。」

Notes

immortal [ɪˋmɔrtl] *adj.* 不朽的
interfere [ˌɪntɚˋfɪr] *v.* 妨礙
realm [rɛlm] *n.* 領土；國土

Giorgio de Chirico 喬吉奧・德・基里科 (1888–1978)
義大利超現實主義藝術家，是形而上派藝術運動的創始人。

本句原應爲：A work of art must escape all human limits ... to become truly immortal.。
不定詞片語的前移主要是爲了強調該「目的」，在本例中則除了這個理由之
外，也因爲在原句動詞 escape (all human limits) 及其目的之間出現了不速之客
": logic and common sense will only interfere"，爲了讓句意較清楚，將不定詞
片語 to become truly immortal 移至句首乃上上之策。

Dream 12

*For my part I know nothing with any certainty,
but the sight of the stars makes me dream.*

「就我而言，我知道世事無常，但是看見星星就能讓我夢想。」

Vincent van Gogh 文森・梵谷

梵谷最有名的作品之一《星夜》(*The Starry Night*) 所描繪的，就是他所居住的
療養院房間窗外夜空繁星點點的景象。

Dream 13

*Art is nothing but the expression of our
dream; the more we surrender to it the closer
we get to the inner truth of things, our dream-
life, the true life that scorns questions and
does not see them.*

「藝術只不過是夢的展現；我們愈服膺於它，就愈接近事物的內在真實、我們的夢想生活，以及蔑視問題並對它們視而不見的真實生活。」

Franz Marc 法蘭茲・馬克 (1880–1916)
德國表現主義畫家與版畫家，成立「藍騎士」畫派。

本句使用了所謂的雙重比較結構。雙重比較的句型是：The 比較級（主詞）（動詞），the 比較級（主詞）（動詞）。注意，若句意清楚，前後兩個比較級字眼之後的主詞與動詞可省略。例如：The sooner you get here, the better it is. 可簡化成：The sooner, the better。

👍 The Dreamlike Nature of Reality 現實如夢般的本質

Dream 14

They thought I was a Surrealist, but I wasn't. I never painted dreams. I painted my own reality.

「別人以為我是超現實主義者，但我並不是。我從來不畫夢，我畫的是自己的現實。」

Frida Kahlo 芙烈達・卡洛 (1907–1954)
墨西哥超現實女畫家，以強烈的象徵手法展現身體病痛與生活中的情感。

安德烈・布雷頓稱卡洛為「天生的超現實主義者」，但是卡洛說得沒錯，她的現實生活本身就很超現實。她經歷過墨西哥革命、小兒麻痺、九死一生的車禍以及多次不愉快的婚姻與愛情，另外她也因為一場車禍而終生必須忍受苦痛。

Notes

scorn [skɔrn] *v.* 藐視；輕蔑

No one could have less faith in the absolute and definitive importance of the work created by man, because I believe that this world is nothing but a dream.

「沒有人會（比我）對於人類創作絕對而確切的重要性更不具信心了，因為我相信這個世界只不過是一場夢。」

Gustave Moreau 古斯塔夫・莫羅 (1826–1898)

法國象徵主義畫家，以宗教或神話故事為創作題材。

莫羅是法國象徵主義大師，常以聖經及神話中的人物作為畫作的主題。莫羅認為自己在畫中所呈現的是 "passionate silence"「熱情的沉寂」。

Chapter 3

Money
金錢

PEEL SLOWLY AND SEE ▶

Close-up

與金錢共舞的普普教父
Andy Warhol
安迪・沃荷 (1928–1987)

NT$3,000,000,000. That's how much one of Warhol's paintings sold for in 2008, making him one of only seven artists in history whose works have crossed the US$100 million threshold. Undoubtedly, Warhol would have been delighted at the spectacle. Before turning to fine art, Warhol worked at the epicenter of American consumer culture: New York advertising. His iconic paintings of commercial objects like Campbell's soup cans and Coca-Cola bottles were natural extensions of his earlier professional work designing album covers and illustrating advertisements for women's shoes. Warhol, the son of an immigrant Pennsylvania coal miner, grew up loving celebrity, glamour, and "nice things." He painted Marilyn and Elvis (the subject of that $100 million painting). He painted Mercedes-Benzes and BMWs. He was buried with a bottle Estee Lauder perfume. (After his death it took over a week to auction off the 10,000 objects in his home.) He was the preeminent pop artist, someone so fine-tuned to the culture that he was able to mirror it perfectly. Distinctions between high culture, low culture, and commercial culture simply did not exist for Warhol. He said, "Making money is art and working is art and good business is the best art."

3 0 億台幣。這是沃荷的某一幅畫在 2008 年所賣出的價錢，他也因此成為史上僅有七位作品跨過上億美元門檻的藝術家之一。這則奇聞無疑會讓沃荷很開心。在投身純藝術前，沃荷是在美國消費文化的中心工作，也就是紐約的廣告業。他招牌的商業產品畫作像是康寶濃湯的罐頭和可口可樂的瓶子，這是自然衍生自他早期的專業工作，包括設計唱片封面，以及繪製女鞋廣告。沃荷是移居賓州的煤礦工人之子，在成長時就喜愛名流、魅力及「美好的事物」。他畫過瑪麗蓮夢露和貓王（那幅 1 億美元的畫作就是以他為主角）。他畫過賓士和寶馬。他入土時，陪葬了一瓶雅詩蘭黛的香水。（他過世後，屋子裡的上萬件東西花了一個多星期才拍賣完。）他是傑出的普普藝術家，對文化的感觸十分細膩，所以能完美地把它反映出來。對沃荷來說，上層文化、下層文化和商業文化根本毫無分別。他說過：「賺錢是藝術，工作是藝術，好生意是最棒的藝術。」

Notes

threshold [ˋθrɛʃhold] *n.* 門檻

spectacle [ˋskpɛktəkl] *n.* 場面

epicenter [ˋɛpɪˏsɛntə] *n.* 中心

preeminent [priˋɛmɪnənt] *adj.* 卓越的

auction off 拍賣掉

fine-tuned [ˋfaɪnˋtʃud] *adj.* 對……有細膩感觸的

I'd asked around 10 or 15 people for suggestions. Finally one lady friend asked the right question, "Well, what do you love most?" That's how I started painting money.

Andy Warhol

「我徵求了大約 10 到 15 個人的意見。最後有一位女性友人問對了問題：『那你最愛的是什麼？』這就是我開始畫錢的緣由。」

英文用法解析

在他的著作《普普風：六〇年代的沃荷》(*Popism: The Warhol Sixties*) 裡，沃荷曾透露一個他尋找靈感的方法，那就是直接問別人，他該畫什麼。沃荷的確畫了錢。2009 年時他的絹印畫《兩百張一元美鈔》以四千三百七十萬美元賣出。

有個浪漫的畫面是，挨餓的藝術家孤單地在畫室裡創作藝術，而且什麼都沒有，只靠自己的天賦和少許的顏料。每個人都覺得這個畫面很浪漫，然而真正餓肚子的藝術家通常寧可三餐溫飽。從達文西到竇加 (Edgar Degas)，從庫寧 (Willemde Knooing)、沙恩 (Ben Shahn) 到歐姬芙，形形色色的藝術家都有個共同的特質，那就是渴望自由創作藝術，而不必擔心生活開銷之類的俗事。當然還有一種藝術家認為，金錢只不過是達成藝術目的的手段。像沃荷、達利就認為，金錢本身就是十分令人愉快的目的，而畢卡索無疑也喜歡過好日子。還有一些藝術家則是費盡心思要外界注意到，他們認為藝術和金錢是天生的死敵，好比說史隆 (John Sloan)、繆勒 (Otto Mueller)、夏卡爾，以及班斯基。

Money 2

It vexes me greatly that having to earn my living has forced me to interrupt the work and to attend to small matters.

「為了賺錢謀生使我不得不放下工作去做一些瑣事，讓我深感困擾。」

Leonardo da Vinci 李奧納多・達文西

這是達文西寫信給他的金主米蘭公爵盧多維科・斯弗爾扎 (Ludovico Sforza) 的文字。「工作」可能是指 80 噸的銅製騎馬雕像。在下一句話裡他抱怨說：「假如爵爺以為我有錢，那爵爺就被騙了。」五百年後，情況並沒有多大的改變，藝術家還是在抱怨經費！

Money 3

Your pictures would have been finished a long time ago if I were not forced every day to do something to earn money.

「假如我不是每天都不得不做點事來賺錢的話，您的畫很久以前就該完成了。」

Edgar Degas 埃德加・竇加 (1834–1917)
法國印象派畫家，擅以描繪芭蕾舞者的動作來表現光影變化與多元視角。

竇加在 1877 年寫到了這點，收信者是備受讚譽的法國歌劇演員暨作曲家雍・

巴蒂斯特・佛瑞 (Jean Baptiste Faure)。佛瑞本身也是個畫家，並且是早期印象派畫作最重要的收藏家之一。

Money 4

The trouble with being poor is that it takes up all your time.

「貧窮的麻煩在於，它會占掉你所有的時間。」

Willem de Kooning　威廉・德・庫寧 (1904–1997)
荷裔美籍畫家，為紐約抽象畫派，以自發即興式的行動繪畫捕捉人物神情。

在 1940 年代中後期，德庫寧創作了一系列著名的大型黑白畫作，表面上看來是因為他窮到買不起彩色顏料。2006 年時他的作品《女人三世》(*Woman Ⅲ*) 以一億三千五百七十萬美元賣出，成了史上第二高價的畫作。

N o t e s

vex [vɛks] *v.* 使痛苦

An amateur is someone who supports himself with outside jobs which enable him to paint. A professional is someone whose wife works to enable him to paint.

「業餘人士指的是，要靠本業外的工作來養活自己才能作畫的人。專業人士則指，可以靠老婆的工作維生而放心作畫的人。」

Ben Shahn 班・沙恩 (1898–1969)
美國社會主義寫實畫家，以左派政治觀點和線性抽象的圖像表現人道情懷。

班・沙恩的這番玩笑話隱含了他對於勞工問題、民權以及和平的高度關切。沙恩深信，藝術具有引發社會變革的力量。

I hate flowers — I paint them because they're cheaper than models and they don't move!

「我討厭花──我畫它們是因為它們比模特兒便宜，而且不會動！」

Georgia O'Keeffe 喬琪亞・歐姬芙

歐姬芙喜歡畫自然景物（如花卉、岩石、貝殼等），且畫風獨樹一幟眾所皆知。此句乃詼諧之語，事實上，歐姬芙是經過了深思熟慮才選擇以花作為創作主題。

Money 7

I've been trying to sell my soul to the devil for 30 years, and he hasn't even come around to make me a price!

「我已經試了 30 年，想把我的靈魂賣給魔鬼，結果他連找我出個價都不肯！」

George Grosz 喬治‧葛洛斯 (1893–1959)
德國表現畫派畫家，其油畫與諷刺漫畫出自對戰後頹廢社會的批評。

1920 年代，葛洛斯狂野的反權威藝術作品被德國主管當局盯上後，他便移民到了美國，並改採較為傳統的題材與風格來創作。Come around 在此指「走訪（某人）」。

Notes

amateur [ˋæmə͵tʃʊr] *n.* 業餘從事者

Money 8

Liking money like I like it, is nothing less than mysticism. Money is a glory.

「愛錢愛到像我這樣有夠玄妙。金錢就是種榮耀。」

Salvador Dali 薩爾瓦多 · 達利

狂人達利總是語不驚人死不休，說自己愛錢又說愛得好、愛得妙，大概也只有他辦得到。注意，like 可作動詞，指「喜歡」，亦也作介系詞，指「像」。另外，nothing less 負負得正，也就是 something more 的意思。

Money 9

I'd like to live as a poor man with lots of money.

「我想活得像個有一大堆錢的窮人。」

Pablo Picasso 帕布羅 · 畢卡索 ⇨P. 1

根據傳說，畢卡索到餐廳吃豪華大餐時，常會在餐巾紙或菜單上快速塗鴉來抵帳。

Notes

mysticism [ˋmɪstəsɪzəm] *n.* 玄想；神秘主義

Money 10

The idea of taking up art as a calling, a profession, is a mirage. Art enriches life. It makes life worth living. But to make a living at it—that idea is incompatible with making art.

「把藝術當成職業或專業是個虛幻的想法。藝術能充實生命，它讓生命值得活下去。但是如果要以此維生，這個想法跟藝術創作格格不入。」

John Sloan 約翰‧史隆 (1871–1951)
美國寫實主義畫家，屬於紐約的「垃圾桶畫派」，以描繪貧窮地區為特色。

Calling 這個名詞可以指「職業」或「行業」，也可以指「天職」或「使命感」。在上文中，史隆採用這個字的第一個意思，但是他可能也會同意藝術也符合第二種意涵。

N o t e s

calling [ˋkɔlɪŋ] *n.* 職業；天職
mirage [məˋrɑʒ] *n.* 妄想；海市蜃樓
incompatible [͵ɪnkəmˋpætəbl] *adj.* 矛盾的；不能和諧共存的

My art cannot be bought. I will not exchange my feelings for earthly treasure.

「我的藝術是買不到的。我不會用我的感情去換取世俗的財寶。」

Otto Mueller 奧托‧繆勒 (1874–1930)
德國表現主義畫家，作品題材主要表達人與大自然的諧和一體。

繆勒的意思是藝術無價，不可用污穢的金錢來衡量。注意，exchange A for B 指「以 A 換取 B」。類似的用法還有 substitute A for B「以 A 取代 B」。

The Art we look at is made by only a select few. A small group create, promote, purchase, exhibit and decide the success of Art. Only a few hundred people in the world have any real say. When you go to an art gallery you are simply a tourist looking at the trophy cabinet of a few millionaires.

「我們所看到的藝術出自少數幾個菁英之手。藝術由一小群人創作、推銷、購買、展出，並決定其成功與否。說話真正有分量的人，全世界只有幾百個。當你去畫廊時，你只不過是看著幾位百萬富豪的獎盃櫃的觀光客而已。」

Banksy 班斯基 ⇨P. 133
英國神秘的塗鴉藝術家，以挑戰權威及傳統的圖騰驚動歐美街頭。

神出鬼沒的班斯基也曾在畫廊展出作品，但是他把他大部分的藝術作品（有些價值高達 50 萬美元）都留在世界各地的地鐵、街頭、美術館、博物館等的牆面上，而且分文未取。他的作品常蘊含言下之意，留給觀者相當的空間進行思考。

Money 13

Work isn't to make money; you work to justify life.

「工作不是為了賺錢；工作是為了印證人生。」

Marc Chagall 馬克 · 夏卡爾

不定詞 to V 常用來表「目的」，例如：We work to live.「我們為生活而工作。」，但是如一個人是 live to work「為工作而生活」，那他的人生就太累了。

Notes

earthly [ˋɝθlɪ] *adj.* 世俗的；物質的
trophy [ˋtrofɪ] *n.* 戰利品；獎品
say [se] *n.* 發言權

Most art students are generous till it comes to squeezing their colour on the palette. Put as much colour on your palette as you think you'll need and a little over. Don't be stingy with your paint, it isn't worth it. Many pictures haven't become works of art simply because the artists tried to save a nickle's worth of colour.

「學藝術的人都很慷慨，直到要把顏料擠到調色盤上的時候。你覺得需要多少顏料，就多擠一點到調色盤上。不要捨不得用顏料，這樣並不值得。有很多畫之所以沒有成為藝術品，就是因為畫家想省下值不了幾個錢的顏料。」

John Sloan 約翰・史隆

史隆的畫作為他帶來的是名氣，而不是立即的財務保障。從 16 歲起，他就為了養家而去書店和文具店當店員。他還當過報紙和雜誌的插畫人員，後來才去教畫。

Notes

squeeze [skwiz] *v.* 擠；擰
palette [ˋplet] *n.* 調色盤
stingy [ˋstɪndʒɪ] *adj.* 吝嗇的；小氣的
nickle [ˋnɪkl] *n.* 【美】五分鎳幣

Chapter 4

Motivation
動機

Close-up

文藝復興絕世巨匠
Michelangelo
米開朗基羅 (1475–1564)

Throughout his life Michelangelo received many commissions from people it would not have been wise to offend. When Michelangelo was just 16, Lorenzo de' Medici, ruler of the Florentine Republic, asked him to carve a relief. At 21, a commission by a French cardinal in Rome resulted in the *Pietà*, a masterpiece of Renaissance sculpture. When an influential professional guild commissioned him to complete *David*, which would become his most famous sculpture, Michelangelo was just 26. And then the popes came calling. Pope Julius II asked him to create his tomb and paint the ceiling of the Sistine Chapel. Pope Leo X asked him to work on the Basilica of San Lorenzo. Pope Clement VII commissioned *The Last Judgment*, and Pope Paul III made sure Michelangelo finished it. With so many powerful people demanding work from him, it might seem Michelangelo would need no further motivation to work. Not true. Michelangelo cared little for riches or comfort. His apprentice, Ascanio Condivi, noted that Michelangelo was so devoted to his art that he often slept in his clothes and hardly noticed what he ate or drank. Michelangelo was motivated intrinsically, by the specifics of the task at hand. One critic noted that his sculpted figures seem as if they had fought to emerge from the stone. Indeed, regardless of who was paying the bills, Michelangelo was first and foremost driven to draw out the art he saw concealed in nature.

終其一生，米開朗基羅接受過許多他惹不起的人之請託。16 歲的時候，佛羅倫薩共和國的統治者羅倫佐‧德‧梅迪奇就要他刻一座浮雕。他 21 歲時，在羅馬的法國樞機主教的請託下，他刻出了《聖殤》這件文藝復興時期的雕塑傑作。當某個重量級的職業公會請託他完成《大衛像》（後來成了他最有名的雕塑作品）時，米開朗基羅才 26 歲。後來教宗也找上門來。教宗朱利斯二世要他幫他造墓，並繪製西斯汀教堂的天花板。教宗利奧十世要他設計建造聖羅在教堂。教宗克理門七世委託他畫《最後的審判》，教宗保祿三世則確保了他能將它完成。由於有這麼多權貴都向他索取作品，因此米開朗基羅看起來並不需要其他額外的創作動機。事實則不然。米開朗基羅對財富或安逸看得很淡。他的徒弟孔迪維曾說，米開朗基羅對藝術十分投入，所以經常穿著衣服就睡著了，而且根本沒有注意到他吃了或喝了些什麼。引發他創作的力量來自他的內心，確實做好手上的工作就是他最大的動機。一位評論家曾說，他所雕刻的人物看起來彷彿都是從石頭裡奮力掙脫出來一般。的確，不管付錢的人是誰，米開朗基羅都以最強大的企圖心將他看到隱藏於大自然中的藝術給挖掘出來。

Notes

relief [rɪ`lif] *n.* 浮雕

cardinal [`kɑrdnəl] *n.* 樞機主教

apprentice [ə`prɛntɪs] *n.* 學徒；徒弟

intrinsically [ɪn`trɪnsɪk]ɪ] *adv.* 從本質上

> *Every block of stone has a statue inside it, and it is the task of the sculptor to discover it.*

Michelangelo

「每塊石頭裡都有個雕像，雕刻家的任務就是要把它找出來。」

Notes

sculptor [ˋskʌlptə] *n.* 雕刻家

英文用法解析

對米開朗基羅而言，藝術就隱藏在大自然中，所以 What's the task of the artist? 答案就是 To discover it. 也就是說，It is the task of the artist to discover art.。

全心投入、技藝專精、獨樹一格、眼光遠大——這些都是從事藝術工作者的基本條件，但是一般人卻都無法做到，所以大部分的人從來不會認真考慮要拿起雕刻刀或畫筆。因此不令人意外的是，真的投入這項挑戰的人通常都有點自負。假如你跟米開朗基羅一樣，相信自己有辦法用一塊大理石雕出一位天使，或是重新打造伊甸園，那自以為是幾乎就是這個職業的必備條件。藝術絕對是一種自我表現，但是對藝術家而言，它也是一種自我探索。本章第一部分中提到的許多藝術家都十分渴望深化自己對世界的體驗，藝術是他們用來促進個人成長的工具。在第二部分中提到的藝術家，包括杜勒 (Durer)、塔畢耶斯 (Tàpies)、德拉克洛瓦 (Delacroix) 和芬斯特 (Finster)，所展現的動機則非基於個人，而是從社會的角度出發。他們把藝術視為古與今持續對話的一部分，或者純粹是用以讓世界變得更美好的一種手段。狄克斯 (Dix)、布雷克 (Blake) 和達文西所闡述的則又是另一種動機。對這三個人來說，創作的愉悅本身就足以作為動機了。

Painting is not for me either decorative amusement, or the plastic invention of felt reality; it must be every time: invention, discovery, revelation.

「畫畫對我來說既不是裝飾用的娛樂，也不是在塑造所感受到的現實；它必須每次都是發明、發現、啓示。」

Max Ernst 馬克斯·恩斯特 (1981–1976)
德國藝術家，達達和超現實主義的領導者，被譽為「超現實主義的達文西」。

___

人鳥合體、跳舞的巨人、噩夢的景象，凡是看過恩斯特超現實主義作品的人，肯定會對他的「發明」能力驚嘆不已。

 Motivation 3

I often find that having an idea in my head prevents me from doing something else. Working is therefore a way of getting rid of an idea.

「我常常發現，腦袋裡有個念頭就會使我做不了別的事。因此，工作便成了擺脫雜念的方法。」

Jasper Johns 傑斯帕‧約翰斯 (1930–)
美國新達達主義畫家，畫作常以旗幟、箭靶和地圖為題材。

上例中各使用了兩個動名詞結構。在第一句中，having an idea in my head 是 that 名詞子句中動詞 prevents 的主詞，doing something else 則做為介系詞 from 的受詞。在第二句中，working 為全句主詞，getting rid of an idea 則為其前介系詞 of 之受詞。

At the age of six I wanted to be a cook. At seven I wanted to be Napoleon. And my ambition has been growing steadily ever since.

「六歲的時候，我想當廚師。七歲的時候，我想當拿破崙。從那之後，我的野心就不斷地擴大。」

Salvador Dali 薩爾瓦多‧達利

本例中使用了兩種動詞時態。在第一和第二句中，時間皆為過去（當達利六、七歲時），動詞使用過去簡單式。第二句句尾的副詞片語 ever since 表達的是從那時（六、七歲）一直到現在，但由於達利的野心在他說話的「此時」依然「在」擴大，因此必須使用現在完成「進行」式。

Notes

revelation [rɛvl`eʃən] *n.* 天啟；神示

I believe that producing pictures, as I do, is almost solely a question of wanting so very much to do it well.

「我相信像我這樣產出畫作，幾乎只關乎一個問題，那就是非常非常想把它做好。」

M.C. Escher M.C. 艾薛爾

艾薛爾的確表現得非常好。他所創作的不可能結構令人驚異，也只有他的高超技巧才有可能達成。

You have to have a high conception, not of what you are doing, but of what you may do one day: without that, there's no point in working.

「對於有朝一日你可能會做的事，而不是你正在做的事，你必須具備崇高的觀念；沒有這樣的觀念，工作就毫無意義。」

Edgar Degas 埃德加‧竇加

本句中使用了 not A but B 的結構。須要注意的是，A 與 B 必須平行對等，如本例中 of what you are doing 和 of what you may do one day，皆為介系詞片語。

I remember Francis Bacon would say that he felt he was giving art what he thought it previously lacked. With me, it's what Yeats called the fascination with what's difficult. I'm only trying to do what I can't do.

「我記得法蘭西斯 · 培根會這麼說，他覺得自己是在為藝術賦予他認為它過去所欠缺的東西。至於我，我認為那就是葉慈所謂對困難的迷戀。我只是試著去做我做不到的事。」

Lucian Freud 盧西安 · 弗洛伊德 (1922–2011)
彷如繼承祖父佛洛伊德對人類心理的研究，他的肖像畫有透視人心的力道。

盧西安 · 弗洛伊德的祖父就是赫赫有名的精神分析派心理學大師西格蒙德 · 弗洛伊德。盧西安話中提到的 Francis Bacon 並非英國的政治家兼哲學家培根，而是與盧西安同為畫家的另一位培根。

It seems to me madness to wake up in the morning and do something other than paint, considering that one may not wake up the following morning.

「在我看來，要是考慮到隔天早上有可能不會醒來的話，一早醒來不畫畫而去做別的事，簡直就是愚蠢。」

Frank Auerbach 法蘭克·奧爾巴赫 (1951–)
英國表現主義畫家，以重覆重油彩的畫作展現人像與倫敦肯頓郊區風景。

注意，madness 這個字一般用來指「瘋狂」或「憤怒」，有時也可以指「興奮」，在本句中則表示「愚蠢（的行為）」。

Every good picture leaves the painter eager to start again, unsatisfied, inspired by the rich mine in which he is working, hoping for more energy, more vitality, more time—condemned to painting for life.

「每幅佳作都會讓畫家渴望再來一遍，因為他覺得不滿意，而在他所開採的豐富寶藏的鼓舞之下，他希望擁有更大的幹勁、更強的活力、更多的時間——他注定得畫一輩子的畫。」

John Sloan 約翰‧史隆

本句一共出現了五個分詞，其中三個為過去分詞（unsatisfied、inspired、condemned），兩個為現在分詞（working、hoping）。一般而言，現在分詞表達主動、進行，過去分詞則用來表示被動或完成。

👍 Social Contribution 社會貢獻

Motivation 10

If a man devotes himself to art, much evil is avoided that happens otherwise if one is idle.

「假如一個人全身投入藝術，就能避免很多因為遊手好閒所犯下的惡行。」

Albrecht Durer 阿布雷特‧杜勒 (1471–1528)

德國畫家，為北部文藝復興代表人物，被譽為「自畫像之父」。

Devote oneself to 指「獻身於⋯⋯」。注意此處的 to 為介系詞，故其後必須接名詞或動名詞。另，dedicate oneself to 的意思與用法亦同。

Notes

vitality [vaɪˋtælətɪ] *n.* 活力；生氣
condemn [kənˋdɛm] *v.* 使某人注定要
idle [ˋaɪdl̩] *v.* 閒混；無所事事

I feel the desire, or rather the intense need, to do something useful for society, and that is what stimulates me. In every situation I always look for what is positive and beneficial for my fellow citizens.

「我感覺到渴望，或者說有相當強烈的需求，去做對社會有用的事，而這也激勵了我。在各種情況下，我總是會去發掘對我的同胞正面且有益的事。」

Antoni Tàpies 安東尼·塔畢耶斯 (1923–)
西班牙藝術家，為歐洲「非定型主義」創始者，利用現成物及泥土創作。

Or rather 用來引出「更正確」的說法，如本例中塔畢耶斯的意思是：與其說是渴望，不如說是「強烈的需求」。Or rather 也可以用於子句之間，如：He's a teacher, or rather he was a teacher. 「他是老師，或者應該說他曾經是老師。」

What moves those of genius, what inspires their work is not new ideas, but their obsession with the idea that what has already been said is still not enough.

「造就天才、為他們的作品帶來靈感的並不是新的想法，而是他們堅定不移的信念，那就是，之前人們已經表達的還不夠。」

Eugene Delacroix 尤金‧德拉克洛瓦 (1798–1863)
法國浪漫主義畫家，解放僵硬的古典主義，賦予歷史畫面熱血與動感。

Obsession 一般常見的用法是「著迷」，在此處是「信念、念頭」的意思。

Well, as far as I'm concerned, I'm not here to live a normal life. I'm sent here on a mission.

「嗯，就我而言，我來這裡不是為了過正常的日子。我是帶著使命被派到這裡來的。」

Howard Finster 霍華德‧芬斯特 (1916–2001)
美國素人藝術家與傳教士，80–90 年代與 REM 樂團合作而受到矚目。

身為退休神職人員兼素人藝術家，芬斯特的動機來自神啓。有天他在畫腳踏車時注意到手指上有一些顏料，然後他就看到「上面有一張人臉。」接著，他覺得有一股暖流傳遍了身體，並且有個聲音對他說：「去畫聖畫吧。」

Notes

obsession [əbˋsɛʃən] *n.* 擺脫不了的思想（或情感）

Motivation 14

The reason for doing it is the desire to create. I've got to do it! I've seen that, I can still remember it, I've got to paint it.

「我這麼做的原因是我渴望創作。我非做不可！我已經看出了這點，我還能記得，我非畫它不可。」

Otto Dix 奧托‧狄克斯 (1891–1969)
德國新即物畫派成員，以扭曲的肖像反應德國威瑪共和社會的腐敗與戰爭迫害。

本例中連續出現了三次 I've，但是只有 I've seen 才是真正的現在完成式；I've got 相當於 I have to，與完成式無關，在口說時也有人省略 've，而把 got 和 to 唸成 gotta。

Motivation 15

People say, "Why do you paint?" and I say, to make magic.

「有人說：『你為什麼要畫畫？』我說，為了施展魔法。」

Peter Blake 彼得‧布雷克 (1932–)
英國普普藝術家，最有名的創作是披頭四的「胡椒軍曹的寂寞芳心俱樂部」專輯封面。

布雷克所創造的魔法多半是把料想不到的事湊在一起的結果：讓米開朗基羅

的《大衛像》扮成泰山的模樣，馬塞爾‧杜尚則跟辣妹合唱團廝混。

For once you have tasted flight you will walk the earth with your eyes turned skywards, for there you have been and there you will long to return.

「一旦嘗過飛行的滋味，你走在地面時就會仰望天空，因為你去過那裡，也會渴望回去。」

Leonardo da Vinci 　李奧納多‧達文西 ⇨P. 205

本句中使用了「對等」連接詞 for。注意，雖然 for 也用來表示「原因」，但是它所引導的為「對等」子句，因此不能等同於 because（because 為從屬連接詞，引導的是從屬子句）。句首的 for once 原指「僅只一次」，但在本句也具連接詞的功能，有「一旦……」的意思。

Chapter 5

Difficulty

困難

Close-up

燃燒靈魂的印象派巨擘
Vincent van Gogh
文森‧梵谷 (1853–1890)

VINCENT VAN GOGH

Van Gogh knew trouble. After being rejected by his first love, he stumbled through a series of meaningless jobs, until one day he decided to become a pastor. He took the exam. He flunked it. He proposed marriage to a favorite cousin and was rejected again. Van Gogh moved in with a prostitute and her young daughter for a time, but his family insisted he abandon them, and he did. Later, when his proposed marriage to a neighbor was rejected by both families, his fiancée attempted suicide by poison. Van Gogh had contracted a venereal disease. He struggled with mental illness. His paintings from this period are dark and somber. Yes, Van Gogh knew trouble, but those who remember him as "that sad, crazy guy who cut his ear off" are missing the point. Van Gogh's life and work show that he triumphed over his difficulties time and time again. The year after his father's death, Van Gogh moved to Paris, where he met the leading artists of his day. His palette brightened, and it brightened more when he moved to the south of France. The roughly 900 works that he produced in the frenetic ten years before he ended his own life had a profound impact on the development of art in the 20th century. In the hundreds of heartfelt letters to his brother Theo that were left behind we see not a depressed madman, but a brilliant and sensitive artist doing his best to live gallantly in a world that largely rejected him.

梵谷一生遭遇過許許多多的麻煩。在被初戀情人拒絕後，他斷斷續續做了一連串沒有意義的工作，直到有一天，他終於決定當個牧師。他參加了考試，但沒考上。他向最喜歡的表妹求婚，再次遭到了拒絕。他跟一位妓女及其幼女同居了一陣子，但是家人堅持要他離開她們，他也就照辦了。後來梵谷向一位鄰居求婚，結果被雙方的家人打了回票，他的未婚妻也企圖服毒自殺。他曾感染過性病，並患有精神病。他在這段時間的畫作既晦暗又陰鬱。的確，梵谷碰到許多麻煩，但是許多人並沒有抓到重點，只記得他是「那個把自己的耳朵割下來的悲慘瘋子」。梵谷的生活和工作顯示，他一再地克服各種難關。在父親過世的第二年，梵谷搬到巴黎並認識了當時的頂尖藝術家。他的用色變得很鮮明，當他再度遷居法國南部，他的用色變得更為明亮。在他自我了斷前那發狂似的十年間，他產出了大約 900 件作品，並對 20 世紀的藝術發展造成了極深遠的影響。在數百封流傳下來寫給弟弟提奧的感人信件中，我們看到的不是個憂鬱的瘋子，而是個優秀又敏感的藝術家，竭盡全力勇敢地活在一個總是拒絕他的世界。

Notes

stumble [ˈstʌmbl] v. 使絆倒
prostitute [ˈprɑstə‚tjut] n. 娼妓
contract [kənˈtrækt] v. 得（病）
venereal [vəˈnɪrɪəl] disease n. 性病
somber [ˈsɑmbə] adj. 昏暗的；陰沉的

palette [ˈpælɪt] n.（畫作或畫家的）用色
frenetic [frɪˈnɛtɪk] adj. 發狂似的
heartfelt [ˈhɑrt‚fɛlt] adj. 真誠的
gallantly [ˈgæləntlɪ] adv. 勇敢的

> ***The fishermen know that the sea is dangerous and the storm terrible, but they have never found these dangers sufficient reason for remaining ashore.***

Vincent van Gogh

「漁夫們都知道大海的危險、暴風的可怕，但是他們從來不認為這些危險足以成為留在岸上的理由。」

本句的 danger 有兩種用法。文中把 danger 當作可數名詞用，因此出現複數形。但有時 danger 作不可數名詞用，例如：The patient is out of danger now.「病人現在已脫離險境。」，或如下一個引用句中的 in the midst of danger「處於危險之中」。

本章覽導

本章的頭幾句名言皆出自文森・梵谷。令人印象深刻的除了他在面對麻煩時所做的坦率描述之外，還有他在面對這些困難時表現出的無比樂觀。梵谷的堅毅在第二部分獲得了歐姬芙、畢卡索、達文西和雷諾瓦 (Renoir) 的迴響，他們在遭遇迎面而來的困難時，都能坦然以對然後各個擊破。對於其他的幾個藝術家，包括德庫寧、達利、勞森柏格 (Rouschberg) 和勒弗 (Lover)，而言，困難為藝術家帶來的則是珍貴的經驗。最後一部分中卡洛和尼爾 (Neel) 在面對困難時，靠的是他們的才華和冷面笑匠式的幽默機智。

Difficulty 2

I feel a certain calm. There is safety in the midst of danger. What would life be if we had no courage to attempt anything? It will be a hard pull for me; the tide rises high, almost to the lips and perhaps higher still, how can I know? But I shall fight my battle, and sell my life dearly, and try to win and get the best of it.

「我感受到是種平靜。危險當中亦有安全。假如我們沒有勇氣去嘗試任何事，人生會是什麼樣子？對我來說，那將是個難關；潮水升高，就快要淹到唇邊，也許還會升得更高，我怎麼知道？但是我會挺身奮戰，讓自己的犧牲有價值，努力爭取勝利，並獲得最好的結果。」

Vincent van Gogh　文森・梵谷 ⇨P. 59

如前所述，梵谷的一生充滿了困難，但是他卻能咬牙度過各種難關，雖然在世時沒得到應有的重視，死後終於為世人認可。上文中的 pull 原意是「費力的前進」，a hard pull 就是「須奮力通過的難關」。

Notes

dearly [ˋdɪrlɪ] *adv.* 付出巨大代價地；昂貴地

If you hear a voice within you say "you cannot paint," then by all means paint, and that voice will be silenced.

「假如你聽到心裡有個聲音對你說『你不會畫』，那就該不顧一切地去畫，那個聲音就會安靜下來。」

Vincent van Gogh 文森‧梵谷 ⇨P. 59

By all means 指「盡一切辦法」。注意 means「方法、手段」為單、複數同形字，例如：one means「一個方法」、many means「許多方法」。相關的用語還有：by no means「決不」、The end justifies the means.「為達目的，不擇手段」。

As we advance in life it becomes more and more difficult, but in fighting the difficulties the inmost strength of the heart is developed.

「隨著我們年歲的增長，人生會變得愈來愈困難，但是在克服困難時，內心也會培養出最深層的力量。」

Vincent van Gogh 文森‧梵谷 ⇨P. 59

梵谷最令人敬佩之處並非他的繪畫天賦，而是他對人生或生命的體會，明知人生的道路充滿崎嶇，他還是勇敢地走下去，縱使日後生命是以悲劇收場。

Notes

inmost [ˋɪn͵most] *adj.* 最深處的

It constantly remains a source of disappointment to me that my drawings are not yet what I want them to be. The difficulties are indeed numerous and great, and cannot be overcome at once. To make progress is a kind of miner's work; it doesn't advance as quickly as one would like, and as others also expect, but as one stands before such a task, the basic necessities are patience and faithfulness. In fact, I do not think much about the difficulties, because if one thought of them too much one would get stunned or disturbed.

「我的失望來源始終在於我的畫一直達不到我想要的樣子。困難確實又多又大，一下子也克服不了。進步是一種宛如礦工的工作；它的進展不會如你所希望或他人期待地那麼快，可是當你面對這樣的工作時，耐心和堅貞是基本的必要條件。事實上，對於困難我並不會多想，因為要是想太多，就會被嚇倒或受到干擾。」

Vincent van Gogh　文森‧梵谷 ⇨P. 59

上文節錄自寫給弟弟提奧的信，日期爲 1883 年 3 月。梵谷直到快 30 歲時才開始畫畫，而且在此不到三年前，他才上了第一堂正式的繪畫課。他的第一幅傑作《吃馬鈴薯的人》(De Aardappeleters) 則是在兩年後畫出來的。

👍 Perseverance in the Face of Difficulty 面對困難時的堅毅

Difficulty 6

I've been absolutely terrified every moment of my life—and I've never let it keep me from doing a single thing I wanted to do.

「生命中的每一刻著實都讓我非常害怕──但是我從來不讓它妨礙我去做任何一件我想做的事。」

Georgia O'Keeffe　喬琪亞．歐姬芙

在 single 前出現否定詞（如本句中的 never），意思是「任何一個都不⋯⋯」，例如：I didn't see a single soul.「我什麼人都沒看到。」。另外，keep sb. from doing sth. 指「使某人不去做某事」。

Difficulty 7

I am always doing that which I cannot do, in order that I may learn how to do it.

「我總是在做我做不到的事，這樣我才能學會該怎麼做。」

Pablo Picasso　帕布羅．畢卡索 ⇨P. 1

畢卡索產出的作品有好幾萬件，包括油畫、版畫、雕塑、陶藝，甚至織品，他使用過數十種不同的技術和材料。他甚至曾用特殊照相機所拍下的小閃光來創作「素描」。

Obstacles cannot crush me. Every obstacle yields to stern resolve. He who is fixed to a star does not change his mind.

「障礙打不倒我。各種障礙都敵不過堅毅的決心。有決心的人不會改變心意。」

Leonardo da Vinci 李奧納多 ‧ 達文西 ⇨P. 205

A yields to B 指「A 臣服於 B」，也就是說，「A 敵不過 B」。另，注意第三句話起頭的代名詞 He 指的不是「他」，而是 One，意即「一個人」。

I love those who can smile in trouble, who can gather strength from distress, and grow brave by reflection. 'Tis the business of little minds to shrink, but they whose heart is firm, and whose conscience approves their conduct, will pursue their principles unto death.

「我非常喜歡在困境中還能笑得出來的人，因為他們能在危難當中蓄積力量，並靠反省來增進勇氣。退縮是沒有志氣的人所做的事，但是意志堅定、所作所為符合良心的人則會誓死追求自己的原則。」

Leonardo da Vinci 李奧納多 · 達文西 ⇨P. 205

第二句話句首的 'Tis [tiz] 指 It is，在古文或古詩裡常見；句尾 unto death 指的是 until death，unto [ˋʌntʊ] 亦爲古文。

Difficulty 10

The pain passes, but the beauty remains.

「痛苦會過去，但美麗長在。」

Pierre Auguste Renoir 皮耶 · 奧古斯特 · 雷諾瓦 (1841–1919)
法國印象派發展的重要畫家，作品主要展現女性人物之美。

雷諾瓦晚年罹患了嚴重的關節炎。即使被困在輪椅上，在沒有旁人協助就無法拿筆作畫的情況之下，他還是持續創作出一幅幅的傑作。

Notes

stern [ˋstɜn] *adj.* 堅決的；不動搖的
resolve [rɪˋzɑlv] *n.* 決心

Difficulty 11

You know the real world, this so-called real world, is just something you put up with. Like everybody else. I'm in my element when I am a little bit out of this world. Then I'm in the real world—I'm on the beam. Because when I'm falling, I'm doing all right. When I'm slipping, I say: hey, this is interesting. It's when I'm standing upright that bothers me.

「你知道現實世界，這個所謂的現實世界，只不過是你得忍受的東西。每一個人都一樣。當我稍微脫離這個世界時，我就感到自在。而當我進到現實世界中時，我就是站在平衡木上。因為當我跌下來時，我表現得不錯。當我滑倒時，我會說：嘿，這挺有趣的。只有當我站得挺直時，我才會感到困擾。」

Willem de Kooning 威廉・德・庫寧

Put up with 指「忍受」；in one's element 則指「適得其所」。庫寧要告訴我們的是，人生本來就充滿困難與挑戰，若一切順遂，你就無法成長和進步。

N o t e s

in one's element 處於得心應手的狀態
beam [bim] *n.* 橫樑；天平橫桿

Ah, UNESCO is the most garbage. Any kind of organization for the good will of the people is impossible. It is necessary for the contrary. Young people need plenty of difficulties to achieve something, you know? If you receive a little money for this, a little money for that, everything becomes mediocre, and collapses ig-no-min-i-ously!

「啊，聯合國教科文組織真是有夠垃圾。任何一種發揚人類善念的組織都是痴人說夢。必須要反其道而行之。年輕人要經歷過許多困難才會有成就，你懂嗎？要是你得到了一點錢去做這個，得到一點錢去弄那個，一切就會變得平庸不堪，事情就會被搞得亂七八糟——很丟臉！」

Salvador Dali　薩爾瓦多・達利

達利憑什麼狂妄？憑他是天之驕子？不，任何一個成功的人，包括藝術家，一定得經歷困難和失敗的洗禮才能有出頭的一天。畢竟，不經一番寒徹骨，焉得梅花撲鼻香？

Notes

mediocre [ˋmidɪˌokə] *adj.* 平凡的；二流的

ignominiously [ˏɪɡnəˋmɪnɪəslɪ] *adv.* 可恥地

If you don't have trouble paying the rent, you have trouble doing something else; one needs just a certain amount of trouble.

「假如你付房租沒有困難，你也會在做其他事情的時候遇到困難；一個人就是需要一定程度的困難。」

Robert Rauschenberg 羅勃‧勞森柏格 (1925–2008)
美國普普運動藝術家，利用生活實物和攝影照片拼貼融入畫中。

勞森伯格的這句話巧妙地示範了分號（；）的正確使用方式：在不用連接詞的情況下，必須使用分號來引出下一個子句。分號本身具有「起承轉合」的功能，至於一個句子所使用的分號到底具有什麼邏輯意涵，須視上下文來判斷。本例中，勞森伯格的意思應是：「因為」每個人都需要困難，「所以」就算你付房租沒有困難，在其他方面也一定會有困難。

Circumstances are the rulers of the weak; they are but the instruments of the wise.

「環境是弱者的主宰，但是它們只不過是智者的工具。」

Samuel Lover 山繆‧勒弗 (1797–1868)
愛爾蘭籍的歌詞創作家、小說家與畫家，主要創作袖珍版的肖像。

這句話原應為：Circumstances are the rulers of the weak, but they are but the instruments of the wise. ，因不夠簡潔有力，在連接詞 but 之後又出現介系詞 but（意思為「只不過是」），念起來有些拗口，所以改以分號作為子句的聯結。

👍 Humor in the Face of Difficulty 面對困難時展現的幽默

Difficulty 15

> *I drank because I wanted to drown my sorrows, but now the damned things have learned to swim.*

「我喝酒是為了想要把我的哀愁淹死，但是現在那該死的傢伙已經學會游泳了。」

Frida Kahlo　芙烈達・卡洛
墨西哥超現實女畫家，以強烈象徵的手法展現身體病痛與生活中的情感。

芙烈達・卡洛傳奇的一生遭逢過各式各樣的困難和苦痛，但是她都能處之泰然，展現出豁達的 gallows humor「絞刑架下的幽默」（即「大難臨頭時所展現的幽默」）。

N o t e s
drown [draʊn] *v.* 把⋯⋯淹死

You should keep on painting no matter how difficult it is, because this is all part of experience, and the more experience you have, the better it is ... unless it kills you, and then you know you have gone too far.

「不管有多困難，你都應該繼續畫下去，因為這全都是經驗的一部分，而且這種經驗愈多愈好……除非你被它害死，那樣的話你就知道自己做過頭了。」

Alice Neel 愛麗絲・尼爾 (1900–1984)
美國現代女畫家，創作主題圍繞在朋友、家人、愛人、藝術家與詩人的肖像畫。

尼爾的第一個小孩夭折，第二個小孩則被分居的丈夫帶到國外去。她曾身心受創並企圖自殺，但終能力圖振作重新出發，並且創造了一段很長的成功生涯。如今她被公認為美國 20 世紀最偉大的藝術家之一。

Chapter 6

Creativity
創意

(MNMMX)

Born the son of a wealthy banker, Cézanne need not have created a thing. He could have followed his father into business, or chosen a life of leisure, reading the novels of his childhood friend, Emil Zola, and enjoying all the pleasures that 19th century France had to offer. Instead, he chose to paint. He left his home in southern France for Paris to become an artist—only to destroy his canvasses in frustration and return home in disgrace six months later. He tried working in his father's bank, but the lure of the creative life was too strong. Cézanne moved to Paris again, and this time was fortunate to meet Camille Pissarro. The master painter introduced Cézanne to impressionist theory and techniques, which in turn energized Cézanne's own artistic exploration. Cézanne painted only the most ordinary subjects: portraits, landscapes, still lifes. His creativity was the result of his process: the way his eye reduced those everyday subjects to their essential forms, and then the inimitable way his hand recreated them on his canvas, imbued now with his transcendent observation of light, color, and form. Cézanne famously set out to "conquer Paris with an apple." In the end it was the world that became his for the taking.

生為富有銀行家之子，塞尚原本不須創作，他可以跟著父親作生意，或是選擇閒適的生活，看看童年玩伴埃米爾‧左拉的小說，享受 19 世紀各式各樣在法國所能找到的樂子。但是他卻選擇了繪畫。他離開了位在法國南部的家，前往巴黎去做藝術家，結果卻出師不利，沮喪到把畫作全都毀了，並在六個月後狼狽返家。塞尚試著到父親的銀行上班，可是創作生活的誘惑對他而言實在太強，於是他又回到了巴黎。這回他很幸運地遇到了卡米爾‧畢沙羅。這位大師級畫家把印象派的理論和技巧引薦給塞尚，進而強化了他自身對藝術的探索。塞尚只畫最普通的主題：肖像、風景和靜物。他的創意始於創作的過程：他的眼睛把那些日常主題簡化到最根本的形式，然後用他的手以獨樹一幟的方式在畫布上把它們重新創造出來，他的作品所展現的是他對於光線、色彩和形式獨到的觀察。塞尚的目標是「靠一顆蘋果來征服巴黎」。最後，整個世界都成了他的囊中物。

Notes

canvas [ˋkænvəs] *n.* 畫布

impressionist [ɪmˋprɛʃənɪst] *n.* 印象主義者

inimitable [ɪˋnɪmətəbl] *adj.* 無法仿效的

imbue [ɪmˋbju] *v.* 使充滿；使滲透

transcendent [trænˋsɛndənt] *adj.* 卓越的

Creativity 1

It's so fine and yet so terrible to stand in front of a blank canvas.

Paul Cézanne

「站在空白畫布前面眞好，但是也很可怕。」

英文用法解析

本句中的 yet 為連接詞，塞尚用它來表達 so fine 與 so terrible
二者所呈現出的強烈對比。

塞尚對繪畫最重要的貢獻是，他發展出把自然世界精準地重現在畫
布上的技巧。他的做法是同時呈現兩種不同但幾乎一模一樣的圖像，
即左眼和右眼所形成的圖像。塞尚的超級粉絲馬蒂斯同樣相信，仔細
觀察是創意的首要來源。布雷頓 (Breton)、達利和博伊斯 (Beuys) 則把
創意看得比較抽象。對他們而言，創意就是想像──縱使所想像的內
容很荒謬，甚至褻瀆也無妨。高更和畢卡索強調原創性在創意中的角
色，而葛里斯 (Gris) 和卓藍斯基 (Jawlensky) 則提醒我們，不確定性在
創作過程中的重要。豪威 (Howe) 在社交互動中找到創意的火花；對
夏卡爾、梵谷和克里 (Klee) 而言，創意的起源則較為神秘。

Creation begins with vision.

「創作始於幻想。」

Henri Matisse 　亨利・馬蒂斯 (1869–1954) ⇨P. 191
法國藝術家，以大膽用色與流暢線條引領「野獸派」與 20 世紀現代藝術。

馬蒂斯在家裡掛了一幅塞尚的畫，並深受他的啓發。馬蒂斯（有的人則說是畢卡索）曾說過：「塞尚是我們所有人之父。」，「我們所有人」指的是所有的現代藝術家。

👍 Creativity and Freedom　創意與自由

The man who can't visualize a horse galloping on a tomato is an idiot.

「一個無法想像一匹馬在一顆番茄上奔馳的人是個白痴。」

André Breton 　安德烈・布雷頓 (1896–1966)
法國作家、詩人與畫家，從達達主義望向超現實畫派的領航員。

布雷頓是超現實主義的代表人物。該派認爲，在不受理性壓抑時，創意就會自然浮現。

It is good taste, and good taste alone, that possesses the power to sterilize and is always the first handicap to any creative functioning.

「好的品味，而且光是好的品味，就具有扼殺的力量。它永遠是任何創作機能的頭號障礙。」

Salvador Dali　薩爾瓦多・達利

畢卡索也曾表達過類似的看法：「創意的主要敵人就是『好』眼光。」對達利、布雷頓等人而言，創意就是想像力的發揮，它不應該受到任何限制。

Notes

visualize [ˋvɪʒʊəˌlaɪz] *v.* 想像；使形象化

gallop [ˋɡæləp] *v.* 奔馳

sterilize [ˋstɛrəˌlaɪz] *v.* 使絕育；扼殺

handicap [ˋhændɪˌkæp] *n.* 障礙

I am interested in the creativity of the criminal attitude because I recognize in it the existence of a special condition of crazy creativity. A creativity without morals fired only by the energy of freedom and the rejection of all codes and laws.

「我對於犯罪態度的創意很感興趣,因為在裡面我看到了一種瘋狂創意的特殊狀態。這是一種不受道德約束的創意,一種只靠自由的能量,並拒絕一切規範與法律的創意。」

Joseph Beuys 約瑟夫·博伊斯 (1921–1986)
德國當代觀念藝術家,從事多樣藝術活動,如雕塑、行動藝術裝置。

博伊斯的話為創意下了「驚世駭俗」的註腳,偉大藝術家們不願受拘束的心態在這句話中表現得淋漓盡致。第二個句子省略了假主詞 It 和語意內涵薄弱的 be 動詞。

Notes

code [kod] *n.* (某階級或團體的)規範、制度

Creativity 6

No one wants my painting because it is different from other people's—peculiar, crazy public that demands the greatest possible degree of originality on the painter's part and yet won't accept him unless his work resembles that of the others!

「沒有人要我的畫，因為它跟別人的畫不一樣──怪異、瘋狂的群眾既要畫家擁有至高無上的原創性，但是卻又要等到他的作品跟別人沒兩樣時才接受他！」

Paul Gauguin 　保羅‧高更 (1848–1903) ⇨P. 147
法國後印象派畫家，放棄律師職位，流浪到大溪地尋找生命與創作靈感。

本句中的 public 這個字可作單數也可作複數名詞用，例如：The public is / are demanding to know the truth.「民眾們要求知道真相。」

Art is either plagiarism or revolution.

「藝術不是剽竊，就是革命。」

Paul Gauguin 保羅・高更 ⇨P. 147

對高更而言，一個藝術家的最高指導原則就是要有原創力，東施效顰者難以登大雅之堂。藝術當然不可以是剽竊；藝術必須要創新，而創新就是一種革命。

Disciples be damned. It's not interesting. It's only the masters that matter. Those who create.

「去他的門徒，無趣。只有大師才重要。他們是創作的人。」

Pablo Picasso 帕布羅・畢卡索 ⇨P. 1

畢卡索會把高更列為「大師」之一。高更的雕塑《野蠻人》(*Savage*) 直接啟發了畢卡索的傑作《亞維儂姑娘》(*Les Demoiselles d'Avignon*)。

Notes

plagiarism [ˈpledʒəˌrɪzəm] *n.* 抄襲；剽竊
disciple [dɪˈsaɪpl] *n.* 門徒

Every act of creation is first an act of destruction.

「每一個創作的行為一開始都是破壞的行為。」

Pablo Picasso 帕布羅・畢卡索 ⇨P. 1

畢卡索的「我們不是說『革命就是搞破壞』嗎？」這句話與高更認爲的「藝術就是革命」的想法相互呼應。

You are lost the moment you know what the result will be.

「一旦你知道結果會是如何，你便迷失了自己。」

Juan Gris 胡安・葛里斯 (1887–1927)
在法國發展的西班牙畫家，受到同鄉畢卡索的影響形成立體派畫風。

葛里斯的意思是，藝術家不應預設立場。「不確定性」正是藝術這個領域最引人入勝的地方。

Uncertainty is the essential, inevitable and all-pervasive companion to your desire to make art. And tolerance for uncertainty is the prerequisite to succeeding.

「不確定必定無可避免且無孔不入地伴隨著你對於創作藝術的渴望。忍受不確定則是成功的先決條件。」

Alexej von Jawlensky 亞歷克謝・馮・卓藍斯基 (1864–1941)
俄國表現主義畫家，活躍於德國，為新慕尼黑藝術家聯盟的重要成員。

對等連接詞通常出現在句中位置，如本例第一句話中的 and。但本例第二句話的句首位置也出現了 And，這是為了避免原句過於冗長；其次，避免由 And 所連接的對等子句與用 and 連接的對等形容詞混淆不清。事實上，若不考慮句子長短，在第二個子句 And 之前打逗號，即可避免第二種困擾。

👍 **The Creative Impulse** 創作衝動

Creativity is supposed to open your world up to others, to the world itself. It's a funny mix, I think, but it must be a happy one.

「創意應該是對他人、對這個世界本身敞開你的世界。我認為這是個有趣的組合，但也必須是個快樂的組合。」

John Howe　約翰‧豪威 (1957–)
加拿大插畫家及奇幻藝術家，最為人所知的作品為《魔戒》。

約翰‧豪威是個奇幻插畫家，他最有名的就是在《魔戒》（包含書和電影）裡的創作。他提出了有別於其他藝術家的觀點。身為通俗創作藝術家，豪威把他的創意作品視為雙向的溝通管道。

Creativity 13

If I create from the heart, nearly everything works; if from the head, almost nothing.

「假如我的創作發自內心，幾乎就會無往不利；假如是發自腦袋，幾乎就會一事無成。」

Marc Chagall　馬克‧夏卡爾

本句使用了分號連結了兩個結構相同的複雜句；但因為前後兩個複雜句的結構相同，所以分號後之複雜句中的從屬子句（if 子句）和主要子句都使用了省略，原句應為：If (I create) from the head, almost nothing (works)。

Notes

inevitable [ɪn`ɛvətəbl] *adj.* 無可避免的；必然發生的
all-pervasive [`ɔlpɚ`vesɪv] *adj.* 無孔不入的
prerequisite [ˌpri`rɛkwəzɪt] *n.* 必要條件

> *I can very well do without God both in my life and in my painting, but I cannot, suffering as I am, do without something which is greater than I am, which is my life, the power to create.*

「在我的人生和我的畫作裡，我都大可不需要上帝，但是痛苦如我，我少不了比我強大的東西，那就是我的生命，就是創作的力量。」

Vincent van Gogh　文森・梵谷 ⇨P. 59

本句的結構看起來相當複雜，一共出現了五個逗號，六個動詞（也就是六個子句）。事實上，梵谷主要要說的是：I can do without God, but I cannot do without the power to create.。

> *The creative impulse suddenly springs to life, like a flame, passes through the hand on to the canvas, where it spreads farther until, like the spark that closes an electric circuit, it returns to the source: the eye and the mind.*

「創作的衝勁突然湧現，像火焰一樣，從手中傳到畫布上，並在畫布上擴散開來，直到像關閉電路的火花一樣，它回到了源頭：眼睛和腦海。」

Paul Klee　保羅・克里 (1879–1940)

主張「讓線條去散步」的德國包浩斯設計師、藝術家與藝術教育者。

克里在這個句子中用他獨特的比喻方式來表達他對創意的看法：創意就像火焰，也像火花。可惜他沒有說明他的創作之火是怎麼來的。對他而言，這或許是渾然天成，是一種天賦。

Chapter 7

Ability
才能

Close-up

抽象表現主義先驅
Jackson Pollock
傑克森·波洛克
(1912–1956)

In November 2006, the auction house Southeby's brokered the sale of a painting by American abstract expressionist painter Jackson Pollock. Since its founding in 1744, Southeby's has moved thousands of paintings, but this particular sale was notable for the price tag, a cool $140 million, making it the most expensive piece of art ever purchased. Ever. In the history of the world. And all that money for a work in a style that many critics have described as chaotic, meaningless, brainless, and idiotic. The painting, *No. 5, 1948*, is dizzying. To create it, Pollock laid a 240 x 120 cm. sheet of fiberboard on the floor and danced around it while dripping, drizzling, pouring, splashing, and flinging brown and yellow paint on it with paintbrushes, sticks, knives, and who knows what else. Layered lines of color pile atop one another; they twirl and shoot off in every direction. There is no subject and no center, every inch of it covered in the same twisting riot of motion. For centuries what mattered most to artists were subject, composition, and representation. Pollock disposed of all of these. But why? Were the critics right? Was Pollock just a talentless hack? Pollack himself said, "I want to express my feelings, not illustrate them." For Pollock, the finished work was a simply an artifact of the moment of creation—the act of painting was the real art.

2006 年 11 月時，蘇富比賣出了一幅美國抽象表現派畫家傑克森‧波洛克的畫。自從 1744 年成立以來，蘇富比拍賣出成千上萬幅畫，但是這次的標價令人為之側目，高達 1 億 4,000 萬美元，這是史上賣出最昂貴的藝術品。有趣的是，它的畫風卻曾被許多批評家形容為雜亂無章、毫無意義、沒頭沒腦、愚蠢至極。這幅名為《1948 第 5 號》的畫令人眼花撩亂。為了創作它，波洛克先在地上擺了一塊 240 乘以 120 公分的纖維板，然後繞著它，一面用畫筆、棍棒、刀子等等，把黃色和棕色的顏料滴、灑、倒、潑、甩在上面。條條的色層相互堆疊，往四面八方旋轉並散射出去。它沒有主題和中心，每一吋都被同樣的狂亂所覆蓋。幾世紀以來，藝術家最看重的就是主題、構圖和表現方式。波洛克則把這一切都拋到腦後。這是為什麼呢？批評家說對了嗎？波洛克只是個毫無天賦的庸才嗎？波洛克自己的說法是：「我想展現我的情感，而不是闡述它。」對波洛克而言，該作品只是創作當下的手工藝品，繪製的過程才是真正的藝術。

Notes

auction [ˋɔkʃən] *n.* 拍賣
dizzying [ˋdɪzɪɪŋ] *adj.* 令人頭暈目眩的
twirl [twɝl] *v.* 快速旋轉
shoot off（對空）發射
riot [ˋraɪət] *n.* 暴亂；騷亂

Track 08

> ## *It doesn't make much difference how the paint is put on as long as something has been said. Technique is just a means of arriving at a statement.*

Jackson Pollock

「只要言之有物，顏料怎麼上並沒什麼差別。技巧只是把話說出來的手段而已。」

英文用法解析

本例第一句話用了假主詞，因為真主詞 how the paint ... 過長。
另外，注意第二句話中的 means，表「手段、方法」，單、複
數同形。

本章導覽

有很多人第一次聽到波洛克的「滴繪」過程時，自然而然會想說：「嘿，
我也可以如法炮製。」他們當然是大錯特錯（沒有人能像波洛克那樣
揮灑顏料），但這種反應的確點出了一個確切的問題。當我們談到「藝
術才能」時，我們指的到底是什麼？抽象和概念藝術的發展顯示，缺
乏繪圖、構圖和色彩技巧的人的確可以成爲重量級的藝術家。技術發
展使藝術生產出現了前所未見的「民主化」：如今只要是有電腦並可上
網的人，就能輕易創作並分享自己的藝術。長久以來，在畫布上作畫
或刻鑿大理石這種老派的高超技藝已趨式微，但或許正是因爲如此，
它也變得比以往更加珍貴。本章的引語全都是出自不世出的天才，他
們的藝術才能無懈可擊。其中大部分的人在談到自己的才華時，都是
毫不客氣，但本來也不該客氣。他們的作品不僅歷久彌新，而且可能
永遠令人望塵莫及。

Some painters transform the sun into a yellow spot, others transform a yellow spot into the sun.

「有的畫家把太陽變成一個黃點，有的則把一個黃點變成太陽。」

Pablo Picasso　帕布羅・畢卡索 ⇨P. 1

畢卡索一語道出了畫匠與畫家之間的差異。注意，transform A into B 指「把 A 變（形）成 B」。

My talent is such that no undertaking, however vast in size ... has ever surpassed my courage.

「我的本領在於，無論它大到什麼程度……沒有一件事比得過我的勇氣。」

Peter Paul Rubens　彼得・保羅・魯本斯 (1577–1640)
法蘭德斯巴洛克畫派，為宮廷畫師兼外交官，以色彩勝於線條的技法影響歐洲現代繪畫。

Such that 指 "of a degree or quality specified by"，也就是，其後的子句用來表示到達了什麼樣的程度或狀態。

I can't tell you if genius is hereditary, because heaven has granted me no offspring.

「我沒辦法告訴你天才會不會遺傳，因為上天沒給我後代。」

James Whistler　詹姆斯‧惠斯勒 (1834–1903)
美國現代畫家，堅持「為藝術而藝術」，反對在畫中表現情感或道德暗示。

惠斯勒無疑是個藝術天才，但也是出了名的牙尖嘴利。他很少脫離八卦版，所跑的趴也令人津津樂道。

Feet, what do I need you for when I have wings to fly?

「腳啊，當我有翅膀可飛的時候，我還要你們幹什麼？」

Frida Kahlo　芙烈達‧卡洛

本句中的 what ... for 理論上相當於 why；換言之，卡洛的這句話原本也可說成：Feet, why do I need you when I have wings to fly? 但是如此一來就失去了「有什麼用」的味道了。

Notes

undertaking [ˌʌndəˋtekɪŋ] *n.* （負責的）工作、事業
surpass [səˋpæs] *v.* 超越
hereditary [həˋrɛdəˌtɛrɪ] *adj.* 遺傳的
offspring [ˋɔfˌsprɪŋ] *n.* 後代

Carving is easy, you just go down to the skin and stop.

「雕刻很簡單，只要刻到了皮就停手。」

Michelangelo　米開朗基羅 ⇨P. 43

本句有兩個子句，但並沒有連接詞，嚴格說並不合文法。若將逗號改成分號應該是比較理想的形式，但由於米開朗基羅說的是一句「誇張」的話，事實上，在前後兩個子句間並沒必然的邏輯關係的前提下，這麼做不見得妥當。記得，偉大的藝術家是被賦予 artistic license 的。

Talent does whatever it wants to do. Genius does only what it can.

「天賦是想做什麼就做什麼。天才則只做能做得到的事。」

Eugene Delacroix　尤金・德拉克洛瓦

這個世界上有許多有天賦的人，他們也的確能做許多事，但是能被稱為天才的則是極少數人。或許只有像德拉克洛瓦這樣的天才才說得出這樣的話。

Everything vanishes around me, and works are born as if out of the void. Ripe, graphic fruits fall off. My hand has become the obedient instrument of a remote will.

「一切從我身旁消失，作品彷彿憑空出現。成熟的畫中水果掉了下來。我的手成了任由遙遠意志擺布的工具。」

Paul Klee 保羅‧克里

保羅‧克里在告訴我們他具有神奇的能力，他似乎是在替天行「畫」。

Ability 9

I do not seek. I find.

「我不尋找。我發現。」

Pablo Picasso 帕布羅‧畢卡索 ⇨P. 1

許多藝術家把「探索」本身視為目的，畢卡索則提醒我們，有才能的人其實應該把眼界訂得高一點。

Notes

obedient [əˋbidjənt] *adj.* 服從的

Have no fear of perfection—you'll never reach it.

「別害怕完美──反正你永遠都達不到。」

Salvador Dali 薩爾瓦多‧達利

英文破折號之後的部分常用來說明前面的那一句話。前面米開朗基羅的那句話也可以這麼表達：Carving is easy—you just go down to the skin and stop.。

Drawing is the honesty of the art. There is no possibility of cheating. It is either good or bad.

「繪畫是誠實的藝術。騙不了人。不是好就是壞。」

Salvador Dali 薩爾瓦多‧達利

對達利本人而言，他的畫當然是好上加好。他曾說：There are some days when I think I'm going to die from an overdose of satisfaction.「在有些日子裡我會覺得我即將因為過度滿意而死去。」

My mother said to me, "If you are a soldier, you will become a general. If you are a monk, you will become the Pope." Instead, I was a painter, and became Picasso.

「我媽跟我說過：『假如你是軍人，你就會當上將軍。假如你是神父，你就會當上教宗。』到頭來我是個畫家，並成了畢卡索。」

Pablo Picasso 帕布羅・畢卡索 ⇨P. 1

論自信，畢卡索顯然不輸給同為西班牙人的達利。古今中外有自信的人絕對不會想當別人。如何 "Be yourself"「做自己」肯定是一門值得學習的人生課程。

In painting as in eloquence, the greater your strength, the quieter your manner.

「繪畫跟口才一樣，實力愈強，作風就應愈低調。」

John Ruskin 約翰・羅斯金 (1819–1900)
英國維多利亞女王時代的藝評家，與莫里斯同為藝術與工藝運動推動者。

注意，本句使用了雙重比較的省略形式。原本的雙重比較應有動詞：The greater your strength is, the quieter your manner should be.。

Notes
eloquence [ˈɛləkwəns] *n.* 口才

Not every painter has a gift for painting, in fact, many painters are disappointed when they meet with difficulties in art. Painting done under pressure by artists without the necessary talent can only give rise to formlessness, as painting is a profession that requires peace of mind.

「並不是每位畫家都擁有繪畫的天賦,事實上,有很多畫家在藝術上遇到難關時,都會感到沮喪。缺乏必要本領的藝術家在壓力下所畫出來的畫,只會是四不像,因為繪畫是需要氣定神閑的一種專業。」

Titian 提香 (1490–1576)
文藝復興時期威尼斯畫派的宮廷畫家,以色彩和寓言畫受到各國王公們的喜愛。

Give rise to 的意思是「引起……」,在本例中指畫家所「畫出來」的作品。另外,peace of mind 一般指「心安」,在本例中則有「氣定神閑」、「心平氣和」之意。

It is but a poor eloquence which only shows that the orator can talk.

「只證明演講者會說話的口才不算是什麼好口才。」

Joshua Reynolds　約書亞‧雷諾茲 (1723–1792)
英國畫家，將「理想化風格」發揮極致，為英國皇家藝術學院院長。

對雷諾茲來說，才能是達到目的的手段，只是實際創作的起點。

Painting is easy when you don't know how, but very difficult when you do.

「當你不懂的時候，畫畫很容易，當你懂了以後可就難了。」

Edgar Degas　埃德加‧竇加

為了印證他的話，竇加留下了許多在他晚年才開始創作但是沒有畫完的畫。

Notes

orator ['ɔrətə] *n.* 演說家

Chapter 8

Action
行動

Close-up

人道主義攝影大師
Diane Arbus
黛安・阿勃斯 (1923–1971)

CMNMMXI

DIANE ARBUS

Because she was deeply embarrassed by her family's wealth, Diane Arbus was from the start driven to do things on her own. She married at 18 and with her husband started a commercial photography business. Because Arbus bored of shooting fashion models and celebrities for New York magazines, she left her husband and received grants to photograph the people who really interested her: the homeless, the sexually deviant, the mentally disabled, and the physically different—giants, midgets, and conjoined twins. Because the twin-lens Rolleiflex and Mamiyaflex cameras that Arbus used required her to get up very close to her subjects, she spent hours, days, even months getting to know them. Only when they had become perfectly at ease with her would she reach for her equipment and begin shooting. Arbus went out and made happen whatever was required to get the photographs she did, many of which are among the most famous ever taken. Arbus once wrote, "My favorite thing is to go where I've never been," and until her final act, suicide at the age of 48, she truly did lead a life of filled with curiosity, exploration, and autonomous action.

由於家境富裕令她十分尷尬，因此黛安‧阿勃斯打從一開始就想要自己有一番作為。阿勃斯十八歲時就結婚，婚後和丈夫一起從事商業攝影工作。但是由於替紐約的雜誌拍攝時裝模特兒和名人令阿勃斯感到厭倦，因此她在跟丈夫仳離之後，便開始去拍攝她真正感興趣的對象：遊民、性偏差者、心智障礙者，以及生理異常者——巨人、侏儒和連體嬰。由於她所使用的是錄萊和萬美雅的雙眼相機，這使得她必須跟拍攝對象非常貼近，因此她都會花上好幾個小時、好幾天、甚至好幾個月去認識他們。只有在他們能在她面前完全放鬆的情況下，她才會把機器拿來開始拍攝。只要是她想拍的，她就會想盡辦法把它們拍下來，而其中有許多都是非常經典的照片。阿勃斯曾寫道：「我最愛做的事就是去我從沒去過的地方。」直到她在 48 歲自殺的最後一幕前，她的確都過著充滿好奇、探索和自主的日子。

Notes

deviant [ˈdivɪənt] *n.* 不正常者
disabled [dɪsˈebl̩d] *n.* 有缺陷的人
midget [ˈmɪdʒɪt] *n.* 侏儒
autonomous [ɔˈtɑnəməs] *adj.* 自主的

The world can only be grasped by action, not by contemplation. The hand is the cutting edge of the mind.

Diane Arbus

「世界只能靠行動來掌握，而不是靠冥想。手是心靈的前哨。」

Notes

contemplation [ˌkɑntɛmˈpleʃən] *n.* 冥想；沈思

Cutting edge 原意是「尖銳」，現常用來指「先進」、「先端」；cutting-edge 則為形容詞，如 cutting-edge technology 即為「尖端科技」。

假如耐吉是一個人，而不是一家製鞋的公司，那它可能會是個藝術家。談到行動，以下所引述的藝術家全都有個共同的看法：做就對了。沒有藉口（瑙曼 [Nauman]）；別無他法（馬格利特 [Magritte]）；沒有時間廢話（塞尚、勞森柏格、迪士尼）；做就對了（卡拉漢 [Callahan]、波克 [Polke]、約翰斯）；要不然……（布雷克、達文西）。要不然怎樣？要不然你就永遠不會成功（畢卡索），永遠不會被人記得（羅斯金）。這當然不容易（布朗庫希），但是如果你按部就班（梵谷），你就做得到，而且你不能說沒人叫你去做（班斯基）。

If you really want to do it, you do it. There are no excuses.

「如果你真的想做，就去做。沒有什麼藉口。」

Bruce Nauman 布魯斯‧瑙曼 (1941–)
美國當代藝術家，創作媒材涵蓋雕塑、攝影、霓虹燈、影片與行動表演。

在 no 之後也可用單數名詞，當然動詞則須改成單數形：There is no excuse.。

Life obliges me to do something, so I paint.

「生活逼著我要做點什麼，所以我才畫畫。」

Rene Magritte 芮妮‧馬格利特 (1898–1967)
比利時超現實主義畫家，常以引人思考的畫面挑戰觀者對現實持有的既定觀念。

Oblige sb. to do sth. 指「使某人不得不做某事」；若指「使某人負有做某事的義務」時則用 obligate sb. to do sth.。不過這兩個動詞較常用被動式，例如：I was obliged / obligated to do this.「我不得不／有義務做這件事」。

Notes

oblige [ə`blaɪdʒ] *v.* 使人非（做……）不可

Don't be an art critic. Paint. There lies salvation.

「別當藝術評論家。動手去畫。救贖就在其中。」

Paul Cézanne 保羅‧塞尙 ⇨P. 75

俗話說得好：「光說不練，天橋把式。」、「不要只出一張嘴。」，保羅‧塞尙就是個典型的行動派。

I am sick of talking about What and Why I am doing. I have always believed that the WORK is the word. Action is seen less clearly through reason. There are no shortcuts to directness.

「我厭煩了談我在做什麼、我為什麼要做。我始終認為，作品就說明了一切。談大道理，行動就會失焦。直接了當是沒有捷徑的。」

Robert Rauschenberg 羅勃‧勞森柏格

「少說廢話」、「直接行動」，因為 "A picture is worth a thousand words." 「一幅畫有一千個字的價值。」

Notes
salvation [ˈsæl.veʃən] *n.* 救贖

The way to get started is to quit talking and begin doing.

「起步的辦法就是廢話少說，開始去做。」

Walt Disney 華德‧迪士尼 (1901–1966)

美漫畫家、卡通製作人、導演及編劇，創立迪士尼公司，對二十世紀娛樂產業影響至鉅。

以製作動畫聞名於世的華德‧迪士尼之所以能成功，就是深知「坐而言不如起而行」的道理。

In terms of art, the only real answer that I know of is to do it. If you don't do it, you don't know what might happen.

「就藝術的角度而言，我知道的唯一答案就是動手去做。如果你不去做，就不知道會發生什麼事。」

Harry Callahan 哈利‧卡拉漢 (1912–1943)

美國攝影師，擅於將平凡的地景行人或妻子肖像化為驚人的攝影構圖表現。

卡拉漢說到做到。他每天早上都會到附近散步、拍照。每天下午就回家把最好的照片洗出來。結果是：他成了當代最受推崇的攝影師之一。

We cannot rely on it that good painting will be made one day. We have to take the matter in hand ourselves.

「我們不能指望好畫總有一天會被創作出來。我們必須親自動手把它畫出來。」

Sigmar Polke 席格瑪‧波克 (1941–2010)
德國畫家與攝影師,以多變的風格與材料創作記錄德國社會文化的變遷。

波克在句尾用了反身代名詞 ourselves,目的就是要強調「我們本身」;換言之,他認為「我們」必須「身體力行」。

Take something. Do something to it. Do something else to it.

「找樣東西,對它做點什麼,再多做點什麼。」

Jasper Johns 傑斯帕‧約翰斯

約翰斯這三句話要傳達的訊息再明確不過了,那就是:"Just do it."。

He who desires, but acts not, breeds pestilence.

「渴望但不行動的人會造成危害。」

William Blake 威廉・布雷克 (1757–1827) ⇨P. 161
英國浪漫主義時期的詩人、畫家與版畫家，表現詩畫合一的宇宙先覺經驗。

這句話有「文言文」的味道。的確，布雷克除了是位藝術家外也是位詩人。
換成較白話的說法應是：One who desires but does not act breeds pestilence.。

Action 11

Iron rusts from disuse; stagnant water loses its purity and in cold weather becomes frozen; even so does inaction sap the vigor of the mind.

「鐵不用就會生鏽；水不動就會失去純淨，在冷時天還會結冰；毫無作為更是會消耗心靈的活力。」

Leonardo da Vinci 李奧納多・達文西 ⇨P. 205

「戶樞不蠹，流水不腐」，一個不採取行動、毫無作為的人是不可能成功的。

Notes

pestilence [ˋpɛstḷəns] *n.* 瘟疫；有害的事物　　sap [sæp] *v.* 使元氣大傷
stagnant [ˋstægnənt] *adj.* 不流動的　　vigor [ˋvɪgɚ] *n.* 活力

Action 12

Action is the foundational key to all success.

「行動是一切成功的根本關鍵。」

Pablo Picasso 帕布羅‧畢卡索 ⇨P. 1

畢卡索絕不是個懶散的人（參見第一章）。他曾說過："Give me a museum and I'll fill it!"「給我一座博物館，我就會把它塞滿！」，以及 "Only put off until tomorrow what you are willing to die having left undone."「只有你寧死也不做的事才需要拖到明天。」。

Action 13

What we think, or what we know, or what we believe is, in the end, of little consequence. The only consequence is what we do.

「我們想什麼、知道什麼或相信什麼到最後都不會有結果。唯一有的結果是我們做了什麼。」

John Ruskin 約翰‧羅斯金

本例第一句話的主詞為三個名詞子句：What we think、what we know、what we believe。但是，當主詞為 A or B (or C or ...) 的形式時，動詞必須和最靠近動詞的那一項一致。以本句為例，最靠近動詞的一項為 what we believe，因 what we believe 為一名詞子句，而名詞子句一律視為單數名詞，故動詞用 is。

To see far is one thing, going there is another.

「看得遠是一回事，走到那裡是另一回事。」

Constantin Brâncuşi　康士坦丁・布朗庫希 (1876–1957)
成名於法國的羅馬尼亞雕塑家，作品多為與時代結合的戶外大型紀念碑。

布朗庫希所要畫的不是外形，而是「事物的本質」。他所背負的這個艱鉅任務的確需要走很遠才能達成。他的方法很簡單：「工作時像個奴隸，統馭時像個國王，創作時像個上帝。」

Great things are not done by impulse, but by a series of small things brought together.

「偉大的事不是靠衝動完成，而是靠一連串的小事匯集而成。」

Vincent van Gogh　文森・梵谷

這顯然不是一個會把自己耳朵割掉的瘋子的胡言亂語。事實上，梵谷正常的時候比生病的時候要多，而且精神病最令他沮喪的地方在於，只要他一發病就什麼都不能做。

A lot of people never use their initiative because nobody told them to.

「有很多人從來不運用自己的主動性，因為沒有人叫他們這麼做。」

Banksy 班斯基 ⇨P. 131

班斯基這句話極具嘲諷的意味。一個人既然有「主動性」，又何須聽命他人的指示？

Notes

initiative [ɪˈnɪʃətɪv] *n.* 主動的行動；主動性

Chapter 9

Attitude
態度

Close-up

用相機記錄歷史的攝影大師
Henri Cartier-Bresson
亨利‧卡蒂埃—布勒松
(1908–2004)

HENRI CARTIER-BRESSON

"To be present, to be sensitive, and to participate" is how Cartier-Bresson described his attitude toward his work and his life. Generally acclaimed as the greatest photographer of the 20th century, Cartier-Bresson was indeed present at the great events of his generation. After escaping from a Nazi prison camp, he dug up a camera he had buried in a field before the war and used it to document the French Resistance and the liberation of Paris. He was with Gandhi just minutes before he was assassinated. He photographed the fall of the KMT in China and was in Indonesia during its fight for independence. He made portraits of the greatest statesmen, writers, and artists of his generation. But all that was incidental to what Cartier-Bresson meant by "present." Cartier-Bresson was "present," wherever he was, all the time. As a young man, Cartier-Bresson lived for a time in Africa, where he supported himself as a hunter. After returning to Paris, this man who had patiently tracked and shot game picked up a camera discovered a new quarry. He said, "I prowled the streets all day, feeling very strung-up and ready to pounce, ready to 'trap' life." And that is what he is most remembered for: his perfectly timed, perfectly composed shots of ordinary people taken with a small camera he kept constantly wrapped around his wrist as he walked the streets of the world. Present. Sensitive. And participating.

「**親**臨，敏感，參與」，卡蒂埃－布勒松以此描述他對於本身作品和人生的態度。被公認為 20 世紀最偉大的攝影師，卡蒂埃－布勒松確實親臨了他所屬世代的偉大事件。在從納粹集中營逃出來後，他把他在戰前埋進田裡的相機挖了出來，並用它來記錄法國的反抗行動和巴黎的解放過程。在甘地被暗殺前的那一刻，他就在現場。他記錄了國民黨在中國的潰敗，以及印尼爭取獨立的過程。他為他那個世代最偉大的政治家、作家和藝術家拍過照。但是這一切都只是卡蒂埃－布勒松所謂「親臨」的附帶結果。不管在哪裡，卡蒂埃－布勒松永遠都是「親臨」。他年輕時在非洲住過一陣子，並靠打獵維生。回到巴黎後，這位曾耐心跟蹤然後將獵物射殺的男子這回拿起相機，因為他發現了一種新的獵物。他說：「我整天在街上潛行，神經緊繃，隨時準備撲上前去，『捕捉』活口。」這就是他最令人懷念的地方：他能夠把時間拿捏得恰到好處，他走在街道上時，隨時會用固定纏繞在手腕上的相機來捕捉各種鏡頭。「親臨，敏感，參與」的確是卡蒂埃－布勒松的最佳寫照。

Notes

document [ˋdɑkjəmənt] v. 用文件證明
assassinate [əˋsæsɪnˏet] v. 暗殺
incidental [ˏɪnsəˋdɛntl] adj. 附帶的
quarry [ˋkwɔrɪ] n. 獵物

prowl [praul] v. 潛行於
strung-up [ˏstrʌŋˋʌp] adj. 緊張不安的
pounce [pauns] v. 撲過去抓住
trap [træp] v. 設陷阱捕捉

Attitude 1

For the world is movement, and you cannot be stationary in your attitude toward something that is moving.

Henri Cartier-Bresson

「由於這個世界不停在運轉，對於活動的事物你的態度不可能靜止不動。」

英文用法解析

這個句子連續使用了兩個對等連接詞：for 和 and，但是在 for（表原因、理由）之前並沒有另一個子句，因此嚴格講這個句子並不合文法。若把它改成：Because the world is movement, you cannot be stationary ....，或是 The world is movement, so you cannot be stationary .... 會比較通順，但如此一來卻會顯得平庸無奇。藝術家的言詞總是「與眾不同」，不是？

對於卡蒂埃－布勒松而言，這個世界是許多不斷進行的剎那，有一些值得捕捉並保留下來。時時留意周遭事件的流動使他必須具備不帶成見與不搶鋒頭的個性，而他也樂於盡可能退居幕後。卡蒂埃－布勒松很少接受採訪，也不愛上鏡頭。十分擅長自我推銷的惠斯勒和達利則反其道而行：他們從來不放過讓大家知道他們有多棒的任何機會。倫哈特 (Reinhardt)、沃克 (Walker)、歐布萊特 (Albright) 和羅斯金等藝術家對於藝術和人生保持著相當正面的態度，他們要讓大家知道世界有多美好。夏卡爾、畢卡索和達文西則沒那麼愜意，努力不懈是他們的基本態度。但是藝術家最常表現出來的態度是獨樹一幟的。蘇斯 (Seuss)、席勒 (Schiele)、弗蘭肯特勒 (Frankenthaler)、勒文 (Levine) 和沙恩都談到，渴望把自己的事做好，是藝術家不可或缺的一種態度。

👍 **Confidence** 自信

If other people are going to talk, conversation becomes impossible.

「假如有其他人要講話，就無法對話了。」

James Whistler 詹姆斯・惠斯勒

惠斯勒的自信簡直誇張到無可救藥的地步。他還說過另一句名言："I am not arguing with you—I am telling you." 「我不是在跟你辯——我是在告訴你。」

Every morning when I awake, I experience again a supreme pleasure—that of being Salvador Dali.

「我每天早上醒來的時候，都再次感受到無比的快樂，因為我是薩爾瓦多・達利。」

Salvador Dali 薩爾瓦多・達利

談到自信（或自大？），達利和惠勒斯真是哥倆好。不過自信只是一種態度，或許更值得我們注意的是他們的才能。

Attitude 4

Art is too serious to be taken seriously.

「藝術太嚴肅了，所以不能嚴肅以待。」

Ad Reinhardt 艾德‧倫哈特 (1913–1967)
美國抽象表現畫家與藝術論述作家，影響觀念藝術、極限藝術甚鉅。

這句話用的是常見的 too ... to ...「太……而不能……」的句型，但是令人玩味
的是 too 之後的 serious 和句尾的 seriously 這兩個字。

Attitude 5

Seven days without laughter makes one weak.

「七天不笑會使一個人衰弱。」（七天不笑就過了一週。）

Mort Walker 莫特‧沃克 (1923–)
以報紙上的連載漫畫「Beetle Bailey」成名於五〇年代。

在畫了 50 多年的漫畫之後，高齡 88 歲但身體依然健朗的沃克正是他這一句
雙關語（weak / week）活生生的最佳例證。

N o t e s
supreme [sə`prim] *adj.* 最大的

A positive attitude may not solve all your problems, but it will annoy enough people to make it worth the effort.

「正面的態度或許解決不了你所有的問題，但是它會讓夠多的人感到煩擾，如此一來你的積極就沒有白費。」

Herman Albright 赫曼・歐布萊特 (1876–1944)
熱愛加州與風景畫的美國畫家，畫作有著亞洲藝術家一般的細緻優雅。

這又是饒富趣味的一句話。正面積極的態度的目的當然不在於使他人感到困擾，而在於使自己樂觀進取。

There is really no such thing as bad weather, only different kinds of good weather.

「其實沒有所謂壞天氣這回事，只有類型不同的好天氣。」

John Ruskin 約翰・羅斯金

羅斯金可不是在玩文字遊戲；他要告訴我們是，不論在什麼情況下都應該抱持積極正面的態度。

👍 Always Try Harder 永遠更加努力

Attitude 8

The dignity of the artist lies in his duty of keeping awake the sense of wonder in the world. In this long vigil he often has to vary his methods of stimulation; but in this long vigil he is also himself striving against a continual tendency to sleep.

「藝術家的可敬之處在於他負有讓這世界不斷令人驚豔的責任。在這漫長的守夜中，他必須經常改變刺激他人的方式；但是在這漫長的守夜中，他本身也在努力抵抗不斷襲來的睡意。」

Marc Chagall　馬克·夏卡爾

由夏卡爾把藝術家的職責比擬成漫長的守夜即可知，他認為一個藝術家一定不能懈怠，必須不斷努力。

N o t e s

vigil [ˈvɪdʒəl] *n.* 守夜
strive [straɪv] *v.* 努力；奮鬥

I'm always saying to myself, "That is not right yet. You can do better."

「我總是對自己說：『那還沒有做對。你可以做得更好』。」

Pablo Picasso 帕布羅・畢卡索 ⇨P. 1

許多人都以為進行式只用來表達某個正在發生的動作或事件，其實，進行式也常用來表示一個持續不斷的動作或狀態。本句的現在進行式就不是指「現在正在說」，而是「不斷地說」，放在 always 之後就更能清楚地表示「經常不斷地說」。

He can who thinks he can, and he can't who thinks he can't. This is an inexorable, indisputable law.

「一個人只要覺得自己做得到，他就做得到；覺得做不到，他就做不到。這是個不會改變、毋庸置疑的定律。」

Pablo Picasso 帕布羅・畢卡索 ⇨P. 1

第一句話的詞序 (word order) 非常有趣，原形應為：He who thinks he can can, and he who thinks he can't can't.，但因句中的 can can 和 can't can't 會讓人覺得非常不順暢（甚至讓人不知道整句話究竟為何意，所以把第二個 can 和第二個 can't 移到關係代名詞 who 前面。事實上，還有另一個方法來避免 can can 和 can't can't 的結構，那就是在第一個 can 和 can't 之後加上逗號：He who thinks he can, can, and he who thinks he can't, can't.。若為了避免句子中出現

太多逗號而產生混淆，可以把原句連接詞 and 之前的逗號改成分號：He who thinks ha can, can; he who thinks he can't, can't.。

I have offended God and mankind because my work didn't reach the quality it should have.

「我冒犯了上帝與人類，因為我的作品沒有達到應有的品質。」

Leonardo da Vinci　李奧納多・達文西 ⇨P. 215

這句話據說是達文西的遺言，而且根據傳說，這是當法王法蘭西斯一世用手臂托著達文西的頭時，達文西對他說的話。無論是真是假，達文西肯定是史上最堅定的完美主義者之一。

Notes

inexorable [ɪnˋɛksərəbl] *adj.* 無法改變的
indisputable [ˏɪndɪsˋpjutəbl] *adj.* 無爭論餘地的

Attitude 12

> *Say what you mean and act how you feel, /*
> *because those who matter don't mind, / and*
> *those who mind don't matter.*

「把你的意思說出來,並照你的感覺去做,因為重要的人不會介意,會介意的人則不重要。」

Dr. Seuss 蘇斯博士 (1904–1991)
美國童書作家及插畫家,著作被譯成 20 多種語言,全球銷量逾 3 億冊。

美國最受歡迎的童書作者之一,蘇斯博士希望各個年紀的孩子都能以有創意的方式獨立思考,而他也以身作則。在《超越斑馬》(*On Beyond Zebra*) 這本書裡,他發明了全新的字母,並解釋說:「我跟你說這個因為你是我的一個朋友/我的字母就從你的字母結束的地方開始。」

Attitude 13

> *To restrict the artist is a crime. It is to murder*
> *germinating life.*

「限制藝術家就是犯罪。這是謀殺正在萌芽的生命。」

Egon Schiele 埃貢·席勒 (1890–1918)

藝術和犯罪對席勒而言並不陌生。他曾因雇用少女當模特兒(並且還跟其中一人同居)而被趕出了某個城鎮,還曾因「在有未成年人的場合中展出色情圖畫」而短暫入獄。

There are no rules. That is how art is born, how breakthroughs happen. Go against the rules or ignore the rules. That is what invention is about.

「無視於規則。藝術就是這樣誕生的,突破就是這樣出現的。打破規則或別管規則。發明就是這麼一回事。」

Helen Frankenthaler 海倫・弗蘭肯特勒 (1928–)
美國抽象派畫家,受行動藝術家波洛克影響,以抽象大色塊表現情感。

弗蘭肯特勒認為藝術就是要創新,要創新就必須突破。一個只會墨守成規的人是不可能成為偉大藝術家的。

As far as I'm concerned, I want to remain the mean little man I always was.

「就我而言,我要跟以往一樣,始終當個卑鄙的小人。」

Jack Levine 傑克・勒文 (1915–2010)
美國現實主義畫家,常以諷刺題材對當代商業、政治等議題進行批判。

身為尖銳的社會評論家,勒文對於藝術界的浮誇面,例如追逐流行的畫廊展覽以及變來變去的運動與風格,多所鄙夷。他所謂的「卑鄙」指的是強硬和堅持,而不是下流與冷血。

Notes

germinating [ˋdʒɝməˌnetɪŋ] *adj.* 正在萌芽的　　mean [min] *adj.* 卑鄙的

Art almost always has its ingredient of impudence, its flouting of established authority, so that it may substitute its own authority, and its own enlightenment.

「藝術幾乎總是帶有目中無人的色彩和對既有權威的蔑視，如此它就可以取代自身的權威以及對自身的啟發。」

Ben Shahn 班・沙恩

能夠自我否定（那怕本身已是權威）的藝術家才能好上加好，更上一層樓。本句中的 substitute 為「取代」之意。

Notes

impudence [ˋɪmpjədn̩s] *n.* 傲慢
flouting [ˋflautɪŋ] *n.* 藐視
substitute [ˋsʌbstəˏtjut] *v.* 取代

Chapter 10

Time and Change

時間和改變

Close-up

神出鬼沒的塗鴉教父
Banksy 班斯基 (1974–)

Much of what Banksy does—painting graffiti on the sides of buildings—is illegal, so it's not surprising that he likes to keep a low profile. Biographical details are both rare and unreliable:

Born in the mid-70s? Maybe.

Grew up in Bristol, England? Probably.

Developed a genius for combining striking images and clever messages in unexpected locations? Definitely.

Banksy started doing freehand graffiti in the early 1990s but was frustrated by how slow it was: he was leaving work unfinished because he had to flee the police—or because he had gotten caught by them. He soon turned to stencils, which allowed him to get his art up in minutes instead of hours. Stenciling and other high-speed techniques has allowed him to create art in unlikely places: on the West Bank wall in Israel, in the penguin enclosure of the London zoo, in Disneyland, and (surreptitiously placed) inside prominent museums like the Museum of Modern Art, the Louvre, and the British Museum. Banksy's work is completed in minutes, but thanks to his stencils it can be surprisingly detailed and extremely powerful. He often makes strident political statements, but his images are usually quite playful. He is staunchly anti-capitalistic, but his art often sells for hundreds of thousands of dollars a pop. He is anonymous, but somehow always in the news. How will these contradictions work themselves out? Banksy is (probably) still young. Time will tell.

班斯基所做的事有很多都不合法，比如說在大樓外牆塗鴉，所以他喜歡保持低調，並不令人意外。有關他的生平資料既少也不足為信：

出生於七〇年代中期？也許是。

成長於英格蘭的布里斯托？可能是。

能在意想不到的地方把醒目的圖案和巧妙的訊息結合在一起？肯定是。班斯基在 1990 年代初期開始從事手繪塗鴉，但是由於速度太慢令他感到氣餒：他的作品常畫不完，因為他必須躲警察，有時還當場被抓。不久之後他改用模版噴印，這麼一來他在幾分鐘之內就能把他的藝術創作搞定，而不用幾小時。噴印和其他的快速技術使他得以在不可能的地方創作，例如，在以色列約旦河西岸的牆上、在倫敦動物園的企鵝館內，或在迪士尼樂園裡。他也曾在知名的博物館，像是現代藝術博物館、羅浮宮以及大英博物館內偷偷放置他的作品。班斯基的作品都是在幾分鐘內完成的，而且因為用模版噴印，所以可以處理得相當細膩而鮮明。他經常藉由作品來表達尖銳的政治理念，但是他的畫作通常相當戲謔。他堅決反對資本主義，但是他的作品往往一幅就要價數十萬美元。他隱姓埋名，可是偏偏新聞不斷。如何消除這些矛盾呢？班斯基（可能）還年輕，我們就等著瞧吧。

Notes

freehand [ˋfriˌhænd] *adj.* 徒手畫的

graffiti [grəˋfitɪ] *n.* 刻於牆上或石上的畫（複數形，單數形為 graffito）

flee [fli] *v.* 逃

stencil [ˋstɛnsl] *n./v.* 模版印刷

strident [ˋstraɪdṇt] *adj.* 刺耳的

staunchly [ˋstɔntʃlɪ] *adv.* 堅定地

contradiction [ˌkɑntrəˋdɪkʃən] *n.* 矛盾

Time 1

Track 11

"The holy grail is to spend less time making the picture than it takes people to look at it."

Banksy

「我念茲在茲的就是，要讓作畫時所花的時間比民眾欣賞它的時間短。」

Notes

grail [grel] *n.* 傳說中耶穌在最後晚餐時所用的杯（或盤）

英文用法解析

The holy grail「聖杯」原指耶穌在最後晚餐時所使用過的杯子
（亞瑟王傳說中的圓桌武士曾追尋過此物）。後人，包括班斯基，
常用這個詞來指「極渴望擁有或得到的東西」。

本章導覽

像班斯基這樣到處快閃塗鴉的人如今會被看作是一位大畫家，或許正
反映了我們這個日益講求速度的時代。在 YouTube 影片的即時滿足之
下，悠閒地觀賞電影的情趣正為人們所淡忘。我們捨書本而就部落格，
捨部落格而就推特，而推特可能很快就不敵臉書「讚」鈕的一聲肯
定。藝術發展的軌跡應該做任何的改變嗎？本節中的藝術家們探討的
是「時間」與「改變」，以及和此議題息息相關的「老化」和「死亡」
等課題。即使現代人對時間的體驗與前人的感受不盡相同，但是這些
大師所表達的觀點，卻已經通過了時間的考驗。

Time! consumer of all things; O envious age! thou dost destroy all things and devour all things with the relentless teeth of years, little by little in a slow death.

「時間！萬物的消耗者；嫉妒的歲月！你那長年的無情利牙的確摧毀了萬物，吞噬了萬物，使它一點一滴緩緩地死去。」

Leonardo da Vinci 李奧納多・達文西 ⇨ P. 205

達文西這句充滿了詩意又極具哲理的話中用了 thou 和 dost 兩個古字。thou dost 換成現代英文就是 "you do" 之意。

Think in the morning. Act in the noon. Eat in the evening. Sleep in the night.

「早上思考。中午行動。傍晚進食。晚上就寢。」

William Blake 威廉・布雷克 ⇨ P. 161

詩人藝術家威廉・布雷克用這四個相當「平易近人」的句子來告訴我們他生活起居的日程表。

N o t e s

devour [dɪˋvaʊr] *v.* 狼吞虎嚥地吃

Time 4

Nothing is a waste of time if you use the experience wisely.

「假如你能善用經驗，就沒有所謂的浪費時間了。」

Auguste Rodin　奧古斯特‧羅丹 (1840–1917)
法國現代雕塑之父，以寫實風格的雕塑展現人類情感，代表作為《沈思者》
(*The Thinker*)。

雕塑家羅丹出身貧苦，他的一生就是一篇耐力和奮鬥的紀錄史。相信也只有
經歷各種挫折與逆境的羅丹才能雕塑出像《沉思者》這樣膾炙人口的作品。

Time 5

The water you touch in a river is the last of that which has passed, and the first of that which is coming. Thus it is with present time.

「你在河裡所碰觸到的水是流過去的最後，也是流過來的最初。因此，
它就是當下。」

Leonardo da Vinci　李奧納多‧達文西 ⇨P. 205

這就是極富人生哲理的話語。達文西要告訴我們的是，每一個人都活在當
下，所以應該好好把握時間。注意，第一句中出現的兩次 that which 可代換
成 what：The water you touch is the last of what has passed, and the first of what is
coming.。

A good artist has less time than ideas.

「好的藝術家所擁有的時間比點子少。」

Martin Kippenberger　馬丁・基朋柏格 (1953–1997)

德國當代藝術家，以多元媒材創作，擅於表現抽象、聳動、滑稽的畫風。

基朋柏格 44 歲時就因肝癌病逝，但是他所留下來的作品卻不少。不曉得他說這句話的時候是否知道天意如此？

It's a great excuse and luxury, having a job and blaming it for your inability to do your own art. When you don't have to work, you are left with the horror of facing your own lack of imagination and your own emptiness. A devastating possibility when finally time is your own.

「有工作做然後怪它害你不能去從事自己的藝術，是很好的藉口和福氣。等到你不必工作時，你所剩下的就是面對自己的缺乏想像力以及空虛。而時間終屬於你自己的時候，可能就會很慘。」

Julian Schnabel 朱利安・施納貝爾 (1951–)

美國新表現主義畫派畫家，曾執導電影《淺水鐘與蝴蝶》(*The Diving Bell and The Butterfly*)。身兼導演之後獲獎無數。

在成為當紅的藝術家暨電影導演之前，施納貝爾早年曾因找不到工作而在歐洲到處流浪，後來還在紐約的餐館當過快餐師傅。

Change 1

They always say that time changes things, but you actually have to change them yourself.

「人們總是說，時間會改變一切，但事實上你必須自己去改變它們。」

Andy Warhol 安迪・沃荷 (1928–1987) ⇨P. 27

美國畫家、版畫家與電影製片，為二十世紀波普藝術領導者。

諷刺的是，沃荷是靠著重製（並藉此微妙改變）過去的圖像而改變了時代。沃荷曾說：" Isn't life a series of images that change as they repeat themselves?"「人生不就是一連串隨著自我重複而變換的畫面嗎？」。

Notes

devastating [ˈdɛvəsˌtætɪŋ] *adj.* 毀滅性的

If we are to change our world view, images have to change. The artist now has a very important job to do. He's not a little peripheral figure entertaining rich people, he's really needed.

「假如我們要改變我們的世界觀，印象就得改變。藝術家現在有件非常重要的事得做。他並非娛樂有錢人的次要小角色，而是真的為人所需要。」

David Hockney 大衛・霍克尼

霍克尼不但是位畫家，同時也是位攝影家，他認為藝術家有責任幫助世人看到不同的世界。Peripheral 原指「周邊的」，在本句中則指「次要的」。

Every change is a form of liberation. My mother used to say a change is always good even if it's for the worse.

「每個改變都是一種解放。我媽以前常說，只要是改變都是好的，就算改變的結果變差也無所謂。」

Paula Rego 寶拉・芮戈 (1935–)・
葡萄牙畫家，於英國畫壇大放異彩，畫作中邪惡場景如故事般充滿想像。

Used to 指「過去常……」，後接原形動詞；有別於 be used to「習慣於……」，後面則接名詞或動名詞。

One of the few graces of getting old—and God knows there are few graces—is that if you've worked hard and kept your nose to the grindstone, something happens: The body gets old but the creative mechanism is refreshed, smoothed and oiled and honed. That is the grace. That is the splendid grace. And I think that is what's happening to me.

「變老有少數的優點——天知道它真是少得可以——而其中之一就是，假如你競競業業地努力工作，有件事就會發生：你的身體變老了，但是創造的機能卻會變得清新、滑順、油潤、鋒利。這就是優點。這是了不起的優點。我想我的情況就是如此。」

Maurice Sendak 摩里斯·桑達克 (1928–)
美國童書作家，為《野獸王國》(Where the Wild Things Are) 插畫作者。

桑達克是深受廣大讀者喜愛的作家及插畫家，著有經典童書《野獸王國》。動畫家約翰·柯里克法魯斯 (John Kricfalusi) 也表達了類似的看法："All artists get better with age. The more you draw, the better you're going to get."「所有的藝術家都會隨年歲而精進。你畫得愈多，畫出來的東西就愈好。」

Notes

peripheral [pə`rıfərəl] *adj.* 次要的

At fifty, that is in 1880, I formulated the idea of unity, without being able to render it. At sixty, I am beginning to see the possibility of rendering it.

「50 歲的時候，也就是 1880 年，我構思出統合的概念，但是並沒有能力實現它。到了 60 歲，我開始看到了實現的可能性。」

Camille Pissarro　卡米爾・畢沙羅 (1830–1903)
法國印象派重要畫家，先後受寫實派畫家庫爾貝 (Gustave Courbet) 與點描派畫家秀拉 (Georges Seurat) 的影響。

從 60 多歲到 70 來歲，畢沙羅持續不斷實驗不同的畫風，包括印象派、新印象派、點描派。

The secret to so many artists living so long is that every painting is a new adventure. So, you see, they're always looking ahead to something new and exciting. The secret is not to look back.

「這麼多藝術家活得這麼長命，秘訣就在於每幅畫都是新的探險。就是這樣，他們總是在展望新鮮、令人興奮的事物。秘訣就是不往回看。」

Norman Rockwell 諾曼・羅克威 (1894–1978)

美國二戰期間的插畫家，繪製無數週六晚報的封面，以寫實的手法記錄了當時美國人民的生活。

Secret 之後常用介系詞 of，如：the secret of their success「他們成功的秘訣」，但也可像 the key to the door「門的鑰匙」、the answer to the question「問題的答案」一樣接介系詞 to，如本例的 The secret to so many artists living so long ...。

Aging 4

It is impossible for emotion not to come on us in thinking of that time now flowed away.

「在想到時間如今已流逝時，我們不可能不受到情緒的影響。」

Paul Cézanne 保羅・塞尚 ⇨P. 75

本句除了使用了不定詞片語（[not] to come on us）外，也使用了動名詞片語（thinking of that time now flowed away）；不定詞片語是本句的真主詞，動名詞片語則做為介系詞 in 的受詞。

Notes

render [ˈrɛndə] *v.* (在藝術上的) 表現；處理

Life is hardly more than a fraction of a second. Such a little time to prepare oneself for eternity!

「人生幾乎連一剎那都不到。人為永恆作準備的時間就這麼一點點！」

Paul Gauguin 保羅‧高更 ⇨P. 147

當高更在還算年輕的 54 歲死於梅毒時，他的兩個兒子都先因病喪生，而他的好友梵谷也已自殺身亡。

Death 2

I don't want to achieve immortality by being inducted into the Hall of Fame. I want to achieve immortality by not dying.

「我不想靠進入名人堂來永垂不朽。我想靠不死來永垂不朽。」

William de Morgan 威廉‧德‧摩根 (1839–1917)
英國藝術與工藝運動的重要推手，以拉斐爾前派風格與花草圖騰創作裝飾瓷磚。

對大多數人而言，能擠身「名人」的行列已是無上的光榮，但是陶藝家德摩根要的不是「名」，他要的是作品能夠永久流傳。

Notes

fraction [ˈfrækʃən] *n.* 片段
eternity [ɪˈtɜnətɪ] *n.* 永恆

immortality [ˌɪmɔrˈtælətɪ] *n.* 不朽；不朽的名聲

Chapter 11

Mistakes and Failure

錯誤和失敗

Close-up

遠走他鄉的藝術冒險家
Paul Gauguin
保羅・高更 (1848–1903)

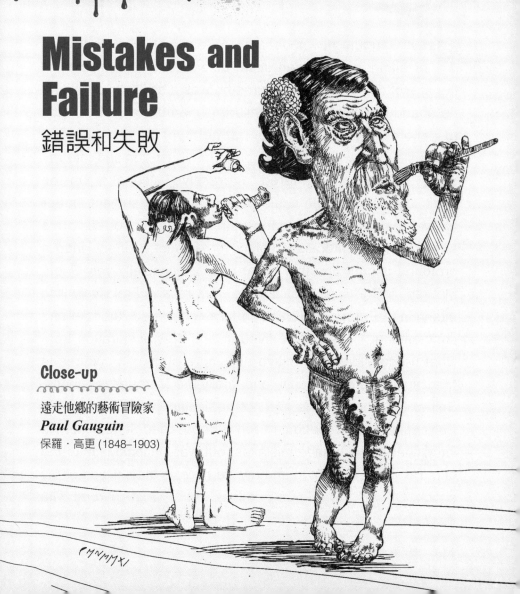

Paul Gauguin never became an old man. He died while awaiting a prison sentence, diseased and penniless, at the age of 54. By most measures he was a spectacular failure: he abandoned his wife and children when he ran off to Paris to become a painter; he contracted syphilis and bragged about sleeping with underage girls (they just "jumped into my bed"); he was self-centered, aggressive, alcoholic. On the positive side, Gauguin could paint. His exotic subject matter as well as his striking style—using strong, distorted forms and striking unnaturalistic colors for emotional effect—had a profound impact on other great artists, especially van Gogh, Matisse, and Picasso. Initially, his work received relatively little attention in Europe (which he in turn considered "artificial and conventional"). Instead he lived in and drew inspiration from what he considered primitive and more authentic cultures in Martinique, Panama, Tahiti, and finally the Marquesas Islands. Self-exiled from Europe and not particularly welcomed by the Polynesian locals, Gauguin lived a debauched, lonely life. He knew that he had made mistakes, but was unapologetic to the end. He wrote, "I want to end my life here, in the solitude of my shack. Oh yes, here I'm a criminal, but ... what's wrong with that?"

保羅‧高更從來沒有機會變成老人，他是在等待服刑時過世的，即生病又窮困，得年 54 歲。從許多層面來看，他簡直一無是處：他拋妻棄子跑去巴黎當畫家；他罹患梅毒並誇稱睡過未成年少女（她們直接「跳到我的床上」）；他很自我、好鬥又酗酒。從好的方面來看，高更懂得畫畫。他的繪畫題材帶有異國色彩──他用強烈而扭曲的形式與鮮明的反自然主義色彩來帶動情緒──這種鮮明的畫風對其他偉大的藝術家造成了深遠的影響，尤其是梵谷、馬蒂斯和畢卡索。起初他的作品在歐洲並沒有引起太多的注意（因此他覺得歐洲「既造作又古板」）。於是他決定投身到他覺得原始且較真實的文化中，並從中汲取靈感；他曾住在馬提尼克、巴拿馬、大溪地等地，最後到了馬克薩斯群島。在從歐洲自我放逐，在波里尼西亞也不怎麼受當地人歡迎之後，高更便過著放蕩而孤獨的生活。他知道自己犯過錯，但始終沒有表示歉意。他曾寫道：「我想要在這裡，在我所住的棚屋的孤寂中自我了斷。噢沒錯，我的確是個罪犯，但是……這有什麼不對呢？」

Notes

sentence [ˈsɛntəns] *n.* 【律】判決
penniless [ˈpɛnɪlɪs] *adj.* 身無分文的
primitive [ˈprɪmətɪv] *adj.* 原始的
brag [bræg] *v.* 自誇；吹噓
distorted [dɪstɔrtɪd] *adj.* 歪曲的

profound [prəˈfaʊnd] *adj.* 深遠的；深刻的
self-exiled [ˌsɛlf ˈɛksaɪld] *adj.* 自我放逐的
debauched [dɪˈbɔtʃt] *adj.* 行為不檢的
solitude [ˈsɑləˌtjud] *n.* 孤寂
shack [ʃæk] *n.* 棚屋

A young man who is unable to commit a folly is already an old man.

Paul Gauguin

「不會做蠢事的年輕人已經是個老頭了。」

Notes

commit [kə`mɪt] *v.* 犯（罪）；做（錯事等）

folly [`falɪ] *n.* 蠢事；愚行

Commit a folly 指「做蠢事」。高更的這一句話（不論對錯）似乎呼應了「人不輕狂妄少年」這種思維。

高更相信，人不犯錯就代表他沒有盡情過日子，而以這個標準來看，他的確是非常盡情地過他的日子。比較理智的達文西指出，清楚的思考可以預防錯誤，但是像瓊恩 (Jorn)、卡爾 (Carr) 和塞尚等藝術家則認為，錯誤和失敗完全不可避免。達利、大衛 (David)、萊利 (Riley) 和皮卡畢亞 (Picabia) 表示，不可避免的錯誤和失敗絕非壞事，反而是成功的必要前提。麥金塔許 (Mackintosh)、皮卡畢亞和胡巴德 (Hubbard) 則更進一步把失敗視為生活中的基本要素。高更的朋友梵谷跟高更一樣，麻煩不斷（參見第五章），但是對於錯誤和失敗他則有不同的見解。

He who thinks little, errs much.

「想得少的人就錯得多。」

Leonardo da Vinci 李奧納多・達文西 ⇨ P. 205

對許多行動派的人而言，「如臨深淵，如履薄冰」的達文西會顯的相當「龜毛」，但對達文西自己來說，「深思熟慮、避免錯誤」才是他的最高指導原則。

👍 The Inevitability of Failure 失敗不可避免

Even the knowledge of my own fallibility cannot keep me from making mistakes. Only when I fall do I get up again.

「連知道自己容易出錯都無法阻止我犯錯。只有在出錯的時候，我才會重新站起來。」

Vincent van Gogh 文森・梵谷 ⇨ P. 59

的確，"To err is human."，只要是人都會犯錯，重要的是跌倒之後是否能重新再站起來。Keep from ... 指「防止、避開……」。另外，第二句話為倒裝句，原句型為：I get up again only when I fall.

To get anywhere, one must choose one's mistakes, I chose experimental acts.

「一個人如果要有所成就,就必須選擇自己的錯誤,而我選擇的是實驗行動。」

Asger Jorn　阿斯格‧瓊恩 (1914–1973)
丹麥畫家、雕塑家與陶藝家,為前衛眼鏡蛇畫派的重要成員。

阿斯格‧瓊恩是激進組織「國際情境組織」(Situationist International) 的創始會員。這個團體包含了藝術家、知識分子和運動人士,他們以創造有別於資本主義社會所認定的生活方式為宗旨。瓊恩所說的「實驗行動」就是在創造這些機會。

Notes

err [3] *v.* 犯錯
fallibility [ˌfæləˋbɪlətɪ] *n.* 容易犯錯;不可靠
experimental [ɪkˌspɛrəˋmɛntl] *adj.* 實驗性的

You always feel when you look it straight in the eye that you could have put more into it, could have let yourself go and dug harder.

「當你的目光直視它的時候，你總是會覺得自己原本可以多投入一點，讓自己放手一搏。」

Emily Carr 艾茉莉‧卡爾 (1871–1945)
加拿大首位後印象派女藝術家與作家，創作深受西北太平洋岸土著影響。

本句中的 could have Ven 屬假設語氣的動詞形式，指「原本可以……（但並未這麼做）」。另外，若把時間子句 when you look it straight in the eye 移至句首，也就是，讓動詞 feel 的受詞 that 子句緊跟其後，句意會更容易理解。

Painting is damned difficult—you always think you've got it, but you haven't.

「畫畫難得不得了──你總是以為自己已經會了，但是卻非如此。」

Paul Cézanne 保羅‧塞尚 ⇨P. 75

本句話中的 damned 是用來強調其後的形容詞 difficult，意思同 very、extremely。Damned 也可用來修飾名詞，如 a damned fool。但是要注意，有些較保守的人會認為這個字是粗話，使用時須格外小心。

🖒 Failure and Success 失敗與成功

I tell you, if one wants to be active, one must not be afraid of going wrong, one must not be afraid of making mistakes now and then.

「我告訴你，假如一個人想積極行事，就不能害怕出錯，就不能害怕偶爾犯錯。」

Vincent van Gogh 　文森・梵谷 ⇨P. 59

這是梵谷在 1884 年 10 月寫給弟弟提奧的信裡的一句話。梵谷在信中告誡弟弟，不可因害怕犯錯而凡事裹足不前，這樣的人只會庸庸碌碌一輩子。

The world is divided into two categories: failures and unknowns.

「這個世界上的人分為兩類：失敗者和籍籍無名者。」

Francis Picabia 　法蘭西斯・皮卡畢亞 (1879–1953)
法國藝術家，起先崇尚印象派和立體派繪畫理念，後轉而崇尚達達與超現實主義。

皮卡畢亞肯定不是沒沒無聞之輩，而他認為他之所以「成功」就是因為他曾經失敗。的確，從印象派到達達再到超現實主義，皮卡畢亞是個具備多種不同畫風的成功畫家，他甚至還投身了電影和芭蕾。

If the work is poor, the public taste will soon do it justice. And the author, reaping neither glory nor fortune, will learn by hard experience how to correct his mistakes.

「假如作品蹩腳，大眾品味很快就會給它公道的評斷。得不到好評或財富的作者將從苦澀的經驗中學習到要怎麼改正自己的錯誤。」

Jacques-Louis David 雅客－路易‧大衛 (1748–1825)
法國大革命時期的新古典主義畫家，以歷史畫著稱，為拿破崙的首席宮廷畫師。

大衛曾經五次爭取羅馬法蘭西學院的羅馬大獎獎學金，但是五次都失敗，於是他企圖餓死自己，以示抗議。不過最後他還是成功拿到了該項獎學金，並成為他那個世代最具影響力的藝術家。

An artist's failures are as valuable as his successes .... By misjudging one thing he confirms something else, even if at the time he does not know what that something else is.

「藝術家的失敗跟他的成功一樣可貴⋯⋯。而正因為誤斷了一件事，他反而確定了另外一件事，即使當下他並不知道那另一件事是什麼。」

Bridget Riley 布里吉・萊利 (1931–)

英國當代女藝術家，為歐普藝術代表，擅長以均勻明亮的色塊或重覆的幾何形狀構成流動畫面和三度空間。

萊利想傳達的意思非常清楚，那就是：我們可以從失敗中學習，因為 "Failure is the mother of success." 「失敗為成功之母。」。

Mistakes are almost always of a sacred nature. Never try to correct them. On the contrary: rationalize them, understand them thoroughly.

「錯誤幾乎總是帶著神聖的性質。千萬不要想去改正它們。相反地，要找出合理的解釋，徹底了解它們。」

Salvador Dali 薩爾瓦多・達利

達利也表達了要從錯誤中學習的看法。他說的「不要想去改正它們」意思是，要面對錯誤、了解錯誤，如此才能有所進步。

N o t e s

reap [rip] *v.* 收割；收穫

> *What am I in the eyes of most people—a nonentity, an eccentric, or an unpleasant person—somebody who has no position in society and will never have; in short, the lowest of the low. All right, then—even if that were absolutely true, then I should one day like to show by my work what such an eccentric, such a nobody, has in his heart.*

「在大多數人的眼中，我是個無足輕重的人、怪人或討厭的人，是個在社會上沒有地位，而且永遠都不會有地位的人；總之，就是最最卑賤的人。好，那，就算這是千真萬確的，那我有朝一日也應該會用我的作品來告訴大家，這個怪人、這個無名小卒的心裡在想什麼。」

Vincent van Gogh　文森‧梵谷 ⇨P. 59

這番話出自 1882 年 7 月梵谷寫給弟弟提奧的信。梵谷終其一生從來沒有大紅大紫過，但是他的作品的的確確告訴了大家，這個古怪的無名小卒心裡在想什麼。

Notes

nonentity [nɑ`nɛntətɪ] *adj.* 不存在的東西；無足輕重的人
eccentric [ɪk`sɛntrɪk] *adj./n.* 古怪的（人）

There is hope in honest error, none in the icy perfections of the mere stylist.

「在誠實的錯誤中存在著希望，只追求風格講究冰冷完美的人則毫無希望。」

Charles Rennie Mackintosh 查爾斯‧倫尼‧麥金塔許 (1868–1928)
蘇格蘭建築師、水彩畫家與雕塑家，為英國新藝術運動的重要成員。

人是不完美的，因為人會犯錯，重要的是要如何從錯誤中學習；一心只想追求完美的人，只是在自欺欺人。

The essence of a man is found in his faults.

「從一個人的錯誤可以看出他的本質。」

Francis Picabia 法蘭西斯‧皮卡畢亞

皮卡畢亞認為犯錯是人類的天性，差別在於「什麼樣的人犯什麼樣的錯誤」。

The greatest mistake a man can make is to be afraid of making one.

「人所能犯下的最大錯誤就是害怕犯錯。」

Elbert Hubbard　艾勃特‧胡巴德 (1856–1915)
美國作家、出版商、藝術家與哲學家，同時也是美國藝術與工藝運動推手。

胡巴德說的一點都「沒錯」，「人非聖賢，孰能無過？」，如果因害怕犯錯而什麼都不做，如何有機會「成功」？

Chapter 12

Education
教育

Close-up

深入人類靈魂的探險者
William Blake
威廉・布雷克 (1757–1827)

CMNMMXI

What could Mr. and Mrs. Blake do with that headstrong son of theirs? He liked poetry and showed an interest in drawing, but he also occasionally saw visions: God might look in through his bedroom window, or a tree might suddenly be full of angels. Unusual kid. They pulled William out of school at the age of ten and started homeschooling. He took some drawing classes and at 14 was apprenticed to the engraver James Basire, for whom he worked seven years. Blake often quarrelled with other apprentices, so Basire got him out of the studio by sending to Westminster Abbey and other London churches to make drawings. Blake eventually enrolled at the Royal Academy of Arts, but formal training didn't agree with him. He developed a life-long contempt for the teachings and painting of the first president of the Academy, Joshua Reynolds, whom he saw as an idiot and a hypocrite. Blake soon left the Academy and began work as an engraver. Blake mastered traditional engraving methods, but is best known for the one he himself perfected: relief etching. This method allowed one person complete control over the production of the art—from design, to engraving, to printing and publishing. The difficult little boy who grew up with visions of angels had created on his own a means to fully realize his idiosyncratic and visionary poetry and art.

對於他們這個桀驁不馴的兒子，布雷克夫婦能怎麼辦？他喜歡詩，對繪畫很有興趣，但是他偶爾也會看見異象：上帝可能會從他床邊的窗戶看進來，或者樹上可能會突然出現許多天使。真是個異於常人的小孩。在威廉 10 歲時，他的父母讓他退了學，並開始在家自行教導。他上過一些繪畫課，14 歲時拜在雕版師詹姆斯·巴席爾的門下，跟他學了七年的手藝。布雷克經常跟別的學徒起爭執，於是巴席爾要他離開工作室，並派他去西敏寺和倫敦其他教堂畫畫。最後，布雷克到了皇家藝術學院就讀，但是正式的訓練並不適合他。終其一生，布雷克都瞧不起該學院的首任院長約書亞·雷諾茲的教法和畫法，並認為他是個白癡、偽君子。布雷克很快就離開了皇家藝術學院，並開始當起雕版師。布雷克精通傳統雕版手法，但是他最廣為人知的是他最拿手的銅版刻蝕。這種手法使人能夠完全掌控作品的產出——從設計到雕版、印刷和出版。這個在成長時幻想過天使的難纏小子憑著一己之力，創造出了一種能徹底實現帶有他獨特色彩與如夢似幻的詩和藝術的方法。

Notes

headstrong [ˈhɛd͵strɔŋ] *adj.* 任性的；不受管束的
engraver [ɪnˈgrevɚ] *n.* 雕刻師
hypocrite [ˈhɪpəkrɪt] *n.* 偽君子
relief etching [rɪˈlif ˈɛtʃɪŋ] *n.* 銅板刻蝕
idiosyncratic [͵ɪdɪəsɪnˈkrætɪk] *adj.* 有特性的

Education 1

Track 13

> *The eagle never lost so much time as when he submitted to learn of the crow.*

By William Blake

「老鷹絕不會耗費一大堆時間屈就自己去了解烏鴉。」

Notes

crow [kro] *n.* 烏鴉

自比為老鷹的布雷克口氣看來也不會比狂人達利小。注意，本句中的 learn of 不是指「學習」，而是指「獲悉」，也就是「去了解」的意思。

布雷克受過各種形式的教育：非正式課程、由父母在家中自行教導、拜師學藝，以及皇家學院短暫的正式訓練。但是除了在青少年時期學過比較技術性的雕版功夫外，基本上他都是仰賴自修（他的脾氣也使得他非如此不可）。因此，他所產出的諸多作品都跟他同時代的人大相逕庭，就算這些人沒有忽視他，也打從心底認為他是個瘋子。布雷克的宿敵約書亞‧雷諾茲主張要嚴格訓練，並仔細研究過往的大師。達文西和康斯塔波 (Constable) 也都贊同這種看法。諾斯科特（Northcote，雷諾茲的學生）和高更以及艾金斯 (Eakins) 都提到了傳統教育的一些侷限。史隆、馬內 (Manet)、傑利柯 (Gericault) 和畢卡索則更進一步表示，教育即便不是有害也可能毫無用處。林布蘭 (Rembrandt)、范伏利特 (van Vliet)、諾爾德 (Nolde)、亨利 (Henri)、甚至雷諾茲本身都認為，對於教育藝術家應該採取務實的 DIY 態度。最後則是塞尚對理想教育的看法。

👍 The Value of Education 教育的價值

Education 2

"Those who are in love with practice without knowledge are like the sailor who gets into a ship without rudder or compass and who never can be certain where he is going."

「熱愛實踐卻沒有知識的人就像是水手登上一艘沒有舵或羅盤的船，他根本無從確定自己會去到哪裡。」

Leonardo da Vinci 李奧納多・達文西 ⇨P. 205

相對於本單元中其他藝術家（康斯塔波除外），達文西相當重視知識的習得，這或許跟他本身是個通才有關。

Education 3

"A self-taught painter is one taught by a very ignorant person."

「自學畫家就是被一個非常無知的人教導的畫家。」

John Constable 約翰・康斯塔波 (1776–1837)
英國浪漫主義風景畫家，畫作以英國東南鄉村水車與草原景象著稱。

康斯塔波讀過皇家學院，在那裡展出過畫作，後來也成了皇家院士。

👍 The Limits of Education 教育的侷限

Learned men are the cisterns of knowledge, not the fountainheads.

「有學問的人是知識的蓄水池，但不是源頭。」

James Northcote　詹姆斯‧諾斯科特 (1746–1831)
英國肖像畫畫家，天分加上自學成功進入雷諾茲大師主持的皇家藝術學院。

諾斯科特是約書亞‧雷諾茲在皇家學院的學生，他後來寫了一本專門討論他這位老師的書。

Notes

rudder [ˈrʌdɚ] *n.* 舵
learned [ˈlɜnɪd] *adj.* 有學問的
cistern [ˈsɪstɚn] *n.* 蓄水池
fountainhead [ˈfaʊntɪnˌhɛd] *n.* 源頭

Follow the masters! But why should one follow them? The only reason they are masters is that they didn't follow anybody!

「追隨大師！但是為什麼要追隨他們？他們之所以是大師，唯一的原因就是他們不追隨任何人！」

Paul Gauguin 保羅・高更 ⇨P. 147

身為後印象派及象徵主義大師的高更肯定不會追隨他人。但是按照他的說法，追隨他這位大師的人肯定不會成為大師。

A teacher can do very little for a pupil and should only be thankful if he don't hinder him, and the greater the master, mostly the less he can say.

「老師能教給學生的少之又少，如果沒有阻礙到學生就該感到萬幸了，而且老師愈偉大，所能傳授的東西通常就愈少。」

Thomas Eakins 湯瑪斯・艾金斯 (1844–1916)
美國寫實派畫家導師，將攝影分鏡技術引進美國並應用在繪畫上。

在艾金斯的這句話裡出現了一個明顯違反基本文法的用字：don't。理論上因為主詞 he 為第三人稱單數，正確的用字應該是 doesn't，但是其實在許多母語人士的口語中卻常用 don't 來代替 doesn't。

Education 7

It takes a great deal of strong personality to survive the art school training. Hard nuts that the art schools can't crack and devour get through and become artists.

「要有極為堅強的個性才撐得過藝術學校的訓練。藝術學校壓不碎也吞不下的硬堅果就能過關成為藝術家。」

John Sloan 　約翰‧史隆

史隆在紐約藝術學生聯盟教過 10 年的畫，他所廣為人知的除了他的畫作之外，就是他能賣出去的畫並不多。他曾警告他的學生說：“I have nothing to teach you that will help you to make a living.”「我教你們的東西沒有一樣對你們討生活有幫助。」

Notes

hinder [ˈhɪndə] *v.* 阻礙
crack [kræk] *v.* 使破裂

You must always remain master of the situation and do what you please. No school tasks, ah, no! No tasks!

「你必須時時都能掌握局面,並做你高興的事。沒有學校作業,啊,沒有!沒有作業!」

Édouard Manet 艾杜瓦・馬內 (1832–1883)
法國前印象派畫家先導,是現代藝術發展的重要推手。

在由現實主義轉變到印象主義的過渡時期中居樞紐地位的馬內,顯然對所謂的教育嗤之以鼻。

Supposing that all young people admitted to our schools were endowed with all the qualities needed to make a painter, isn't it dangerous to have them study together for years, copying the same models and approximately the same path? After that, how can one hope to have them still keep any originality?

「假設來我們學校就讀的年輕人天生都具備了當畫家所需要的一切特質,那讓他們長年一起讀書,臨摹同樣的範本、步上大致相同的道路,

這豈不危險？這麼一來，我們怎麼能指望他們還能保有任何的原創性？」

Theodore Gericault 西奧多‧傑利柯 (1791–1824)

新古典主義畫家，師法魯本斯、提香等古典大師，以《梅度莎之筏》(*The Raft of the Medusa*) 聞名畫壇。

的確，在一個口令一個動作的教育之下是不可能調教出什麼偉大藝術家。第一句中的 be endowed with 指「天生具有（某種能力或特質）」。

Education 10

All children are artists. The problem is how to remain an artist once he grows up.

「所有的孩子都是藝術家。問題在於，當他長大後要怎麼繼續當個藝術家。」

Pablo Picasso 帕布羅‧畢卡索 ⇨P. 1

畢卡索的憂慮也是許多教育改革家的憂慮。齊頭式、填鴨式的教育方式只會扼殺孩子原有的創意和天賦。

Notes

endow [ɪn`daʊ] *v.* 賦予

Education 11

Of course you will say that I ought to be practical and ought to try and paint the way they want me to paint. Well, I will tell you a secret. I have tried and I have tried very hard, but I can't do it. I just can't do it! And that is why I am just a little crazy.

「當然你會說我應該務實,應該試著照他們所希望的畫法去畫。嗯,我告訴你一個秘密。我試了,我非常努力地試了,但是我做不到。我就是做不到!這就是為什麼我有點瘋掉了。」

Rembrandt 林布蘭 (1606–1669)
歐洲最重要的畫家與版畫家,以豐沛的歷史畫作開啟荷蘭的黃金時期。

沒有自己風格的藝術家怎能稱得上大師?聽人指示作畫,縱使能按部就班、依樣畫葫蘆,充其量也只會是個畫匠。

Education 12

I needed to purge myself of all the attention my parents had given me—I wasn't neglected enough as a child.

「我需要把父母給我的一切關注都清除得一乾二淨——我小時候被忽略得不夠徹底。」

Don van Vliet 唐‧范‧伏利特 (1941–2010)
美國藝術家與流行音樂家。

范伏利特是個半路出家的素人畫家,他更廣爲人知的身分則是搖滾樂手「牛心隊長」(Captain Beefheart)。當年他自高中輟學時曾說:"If you want to be a different fish, you've got to jump out of the school." 「假如你想當一條與衆不同的魚,你就必須跳出學校。」

What an artist learns matters little. What he himself discovers has a real worth for him, and gives him the necessary incitement to work.

「藝術家學什麼都無所謂。他自己所發現的事物對他就有實際的價值,並能帶給他必要的工作誘因。」

Emil Nolde 埃米‧諾爾德 (1867–1956)
德國橋派表現主義畫家,擅油畫、版畫與水彩畫,以有力的筆觸和表現性色彩著稱。

注意,第一句話中的 little 是副詞的用法,意思相當於 not much;也就是說,這句話就等於 What an artist learns doesn't matter much.。

N o t e s

purge [pɜdʒ] *v.* 清除
incitement [ɪnˋsaɪtmənt] *n.* 激勵;刺激

An artist must educate himself, he cannot be educated, he must test things out as they apply to himself; his life is one long investigation of things and his own reaction to them. If he is to be interesting to us it is because he renders a very personal account.

「藝術家必須自我教育，而不能由旁人來教育，他必須靠親自嘗試來檢驗事物；他的人生就是一場針對事物及他本身對這些事物之反應的漫長調查。假如他能讓我們感興趣，那是因為他提出了極富個人色彩的見解。」

Robert Henri 羅勃·亨利 (1865–1929)
以紐約生活的寫實畫為主要表現題材，與湯瑪斯·艾金斯等人組成「垃圾桶派」。

依嚴格的文法修辭，第一個句子應該改寫成：An artist must educate himself; he cannot be educated; he must test things out as they apply to himself. His life is one long investigation of things and his own reaction to them.；也就是說，把原來用分號隔開的兩個部分改成兩個句子，而原來分號前用逗號分隔的子句改用分號來分隔。

Could we teach taste or genius by rules, they would be no longer taste and genius.

「假如我們可以按規則來教導品味和天才的話,那它們就不再是品味和天才了。」

Joshua Reynolds 約書亞‧雷諾茲 (1723–1792)
英國畫家,將「理想化風格」發揮極致,為英國皇家藝術學院院長。

其實,雷諾茲比布雷克所評價的要開明。依照雷諾茲的看法,布雷克或許是認清了自己的教育:「在非常大的程度上,學習是永無止境,並受機會所左右;就像遊客一樣,我們必須趁買得到的時候,把我們所能買到的東西給買到手——不管它交到我們手上時,是不是以最便捷的方式,在最恰當的地方,或正好是在我們想要拿到的那一刻。」

Notes

render [ˈrɛndə] *v.* 提出
account [əˈkaʊnt] *n.* 解釋;說明

Education 16

Personally I would like to have pupils, a studio, pass on my love to them, work with them, without teaching them anything ….
The way to learn is to look at the masters, above all at nature, and to watch other people painting.

「我個人想要有學生、一間畫室,把我的愛傳遞給他們,跟他們共事,但是不教他們任何東西。……學習的方法是觀摩大師,最重要的是觀摩大自然,並觀察別人畫畫。」

Paul Cézanne 保羅‧塞尚 ⇨P. 75

塞尚認為的理想教育方式顯然屬於較「中間」的路線。他希望自己有學生,但是他並不「教」學生,而是讓學生自己觀察、觀摩,選出一條最合適自己的路。

Notes
---
pass on 傳遞

Chapter 13

Imagination and Inspiration

想像力與靈感

Close-up

激發創意之火的拼貼大師
Max Ernst
馬克斯·恩斯特 (1891–1976)

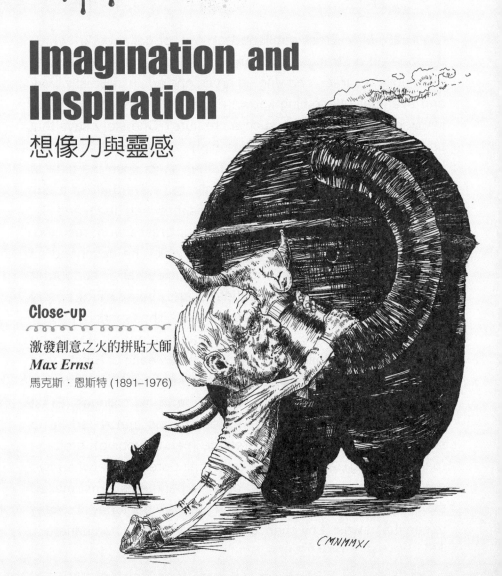

In 1929, Max Ernst published a book of collages, in which appeared a strange bird named Loplop. Loplop went on to have quite a career, showing up again and again in Ernst's work and eventually becoming known as the artist's alter-ego. What inspired Ernst to imagine such a creature? One story says that as a child, Max Ernst awoke one night to discover that his pet bird had died; moments later his father announced the birth of Max's sister. A coincidence, certainly, but nevertheless a link was formed between birds and humans, between death and life, and an essential component of a major artist's work resulted. Ernst was an early master of collage, which he described as "the systematic exploitation of the coincidental ... encounter of two of more unrelated realities ... and the spark of poetry created by the proximity of these realities." The "spark of poetry" is created by chance, but not by chance alone. It has to be systematically exploited by the artist: behind each of Ernst's wild flights of imagination was an artist working hard to create the conditions of their possibility. In addition to his collages, Ernst invented or developed painting techniques that relied in no small part on happenstance: frottage (pencil rubbing), grattage (paint scraping), and decalcomania (paint pressed between two surfaces). Through these and other experiments Ernst invited the spark poetry into his art. Looking at his work today, it's easy to see that it wasn't by chance that poetry found a home there.

1929 年時，馬克斯‧恩斯特出了一本談拼貼的書，裡面有一隻奇怪的鳥名叫洛普洛普。洛普洛普經歷了多彩多姿的生涯，並一再出現在恩斯特的作品中，最後成了這位藝術家公認的第二自我。是什麼啟發了恩斯特去想像出這樣的動物呢？有一個說法是，在恩斯特小時候，有一天晚上他醒來，發現他的寵物鳥死了；不久，他爸爸就宣布恩斯特的妹妹出生了。這無疑是個巧合，但是卻在人鳥之間與生死之間形成了連結，而且是這位大藝術家產出作品的基本要素。恩斯特是早期的拼貼名家，他形容拼貼是「有系統地利用……兩種或更多不相干之現實的巧合邂逅……以及靠這些現實的相近性所擦出的詩歌之火花」。「詩歌之火花」是偶然擦出來的，但是卻不能光靠偶然，恩斯特的每一件作品都因為他的想像力而成為可能。除了拼貼外，恩斯特也是技法的創新者，透過他的拓印法（鉛筆拓畫）、搔刮法（刮擦畫作）和謄印法（畫作壓在兩個表面之間）。以及其他的實驗方式，恩斯特把詩歌的火花帶進了他的藝術中。如今審視他的作品，不難看出詩歌能在其中找到歸屬絕非偶然。

Notes

collage [kə`lɑʒ] *n.* 美術拼貼
coincidence [ko`ɪnsɪdəns] *n.* 巧合
proximity [prɑk`sɪmətɪ] *n.* 接近
happenstance [`hæpənˌstæns] *n.*【美口】偶然的事情

frottage [`frɑtɪdʒ] *n.* 擦印畫法
grattage [`grætɪdʒ] *n.* 搔括畫法
decalcomania [dɪˌkælkə`menɪə] *n.* 謄印畫法

All good ideas arrive by chance.

Max Ernst

「所有的好點子都是偶然出現的。」

英文用法解析

或許好點子是偶然出現的，但是沒有大師高人一等的想像力加持，如何能轉化成一幅幅的傑作？

恩斯特並非坐視空白畫布，等著靈感從天而降。他會把顏料、雜誌剪報和手邊的各種東西拿來把玩，看看各種組合能拼湊出什麼。跟恩斯特一樣，畢卡索、布朗庫希 (Brâncuşi) and 和高茲沃斯 (Goldsworthy) 也都從工作本身尋求靈感和意義。對倫哈特 (Reinhardt)、雷諾斯、克羅斯 (Close) 和哥雅 (Goya) 而言，靈感則不重要，甚至根本不存在，直接動手創作才是根本之道。相反地，畢卡索、雷、馬瑟威爾 (Motherwell)、和伍德 (Wood) 則在他們的周遭世界中尋找到靈感，而梵谷、哈潑 (Hopper) 和達利等藝術家則從內心尋求靈感。

👍 **Inspiration from Work** 來自工作的靈感

Imagination and Inspiration 2

Inspiration exists, but it has to find us working.

「靈感是存在的，但是它必須發現我們在做事。」

Pablo Picasso　帕布羅・畢卡索 ⇨P. 1

畢卡索天賦異稟、產量驚人，因此有人可能會認為縱使靈感沒有找上他，他也會直接把它創造出來。畢竟他就是曾經說過："Everything you can imagine is real."「你所能想像到的一切都是真的。」的那個人。

Imagination and Inspiration 3

Things are not difficult to make; what is difficult is putting ourselves in the state of mind to make them.

「要把東西做出來並不難，難的是要讓自己有心把它們做出來。」

Constantin Brâncuşi　康士坦丁・布朗庫希

雕塑家布朗庫希說的一點都不錯。「無心」做的作品是沒有生命的，有的只是「匠氣」；相反地，「用心」做出來的東西才有「靈氣」，因為它們是創作者精神的延續。

Ideas must be put to the test. That's why we make things, otherwise they would be no more than ideas. There is often a huge difference between an idea and its realisation. I've had what I thought were great ideas that just didn't work.

「點子必須接受考驗。這就是為什麼我們要把東西做出來，要不然它們就只是點子而已。點子和實現之間常常有很大的落差。我就曾經有過自以為很棒而根本行不通的點子。」

Andy Goldsworthy　安迪‧高茲沃斯 (1956–)
英國新時代環境藝術代表人物之一，利用大自然中的元素創作，再加以攝影記錄。

Put (sth. or sb.) to the test 指「使（某事物或某人）受試驗或考驗」。另外，由於高茲沃斯是英國人，所以他把「實現」拼寫成 realisation，美式拼法則是 realization。

Notes
put sth./sb. to the test　使某事／人受考驗

👍 No Such Thing as Inspiration 沒有靈感這回事

> *Only a bad artist thinks he has a good idea. A good artist does not need anything.*

「只有差勁的藝術家才會以為自己有好點子。優秀的藝術家什麼都不需要。」

Ad Reinhardt 艾德・倫哈特

___

倫哈特是抽象派表現主義的大師，他所信仰的是他所謂的「藝術就是藝術」(Art-as-Art) 的哲學。

> *Invention, strictly speaking, is little more than a new combination of those images which have been previously gathered and deposited in the memory: nothing can come of nothing.*

「嚴格來說，發明不過就是把過去那些所蒐集到並存放在記憶裡的圖案重新拼湊出而已：無中不能生有。」

Joshua Reynolds 約書亞・雷諾茲

___

Little = not much；也就是說，雷諾茲認為：Invention is not much more than a new combination of those images ....。

Inspiration is for amateurs; the rest of us just show up for work.

「靈感是給外行人的東西；我們其他人則是直接實地操作。」

Chuck Close 查克·克羅斯 (1940–)

克羅斯特有的作畫方式或許能解釋這種態度。克羅斯是擬真畫 (photorealistic painting) 先驅，他會在大型畫布上先畫出細密網格，然後在數萬個方格上分別作畫，結果就像一張大型高畫質照片。他的單幅作品有時得耗時一年以上。

Fantasy, abandoned by reason, produces impossible monsters; united with it, she is the mother of the arts and the origin of marvels.

「幻想若被理性遺棄，就會產生不可能的怪獸；若能融為一體，則為藝術之母與奇蹟之源。」

Francisco Goya 法蘭西斯科·哥雅 (1746–1828)
西班牙浪漫主義宮廷畫師，以怪誕版畫開啓十九世紀現代主義的先驅。

本句中使用了兩個（過去）分詞構句，而分詞構句通常由副詞子句省略而來，如本句的 abandoned by reason 原本應是 if it (= fantasy) is abandoned by reason；united with it 原本則是 if it (= fantasy) is united with it (reason)。

🔊 Sources of Inspiration 靈感的來源

Imagination and Inspiration 9

The artist is a receptacle for emotions that come from all over the place: from the sky, from the earth, from a scrap of paper, from a passing shape, from a spider's web.

「藝術家是個容器，裝著來自四面八方的情感：來自天上、來自地下、來自一片紙、來自剎那間的影像、來自蜘蛛網。」

Pablo Picasso 帕布羅・畢卡索 ⇨P. 1

的確，Everything is beautiful in its own way.，敏感度夠高的藝術家可以從萬事萬物中獲取靈感和啓發。

Imagination and Inspiration 10

Of course, there will always be those who look only at technique, who ask "how," while others of a more curious nature will ask "why." Personally, I have always preferred inspiration to information.

「當然，總是會有人只看技術，只問『怎麼做』，而生性比較好奇的人則會問『為什麼』。我個人一向比較偏好靈感，而非資訊。」

Man Ray　曼恩・雷

與布朗庫希相同，身兼畫家、攝影家與電影創作者的曼恩・雷追求的不是匠氣，而是靈氣。

Oh, Spring! I want to go out and feel you and get inspiration. My old things seem dead. I want fresh contacts, more vital searching.

「噢，春天！我想出去感受妳以捕捉靈感。我的舊事看來已死。我想要新鮮的觸碰、更有生氣的探尋。」

Emily Carr　艾茉莉・卡爾

與倫哈特、雷諾斯與克羅斯等人相反，加拿大籍的畫家兼作家艾茉莉・卡爾認為自己需要不斷地尋求新的靈感來刺激創作。

Notes
receptacle [rɪ`sɛptək̩l] *n.* 容器
passing [`pæsɪŋ] *adj.* 短暫的；一時的

If you can't find your inspiration by walking around the block one time, go around two blocks—but never three.

「假如你在街上繞一圈還找不到靈感,那就繞兩圈──但是事不過三。」

Robert Motherwell 羅勃‧馬瑟威爾 (1915–1991)
紐約抽象表現主義畫家,在文學、哲學上的表現受歐洲現代主義傳統影響。

馬瑟威爾對於尋求靈感的看法非常有趣:靈感最多只能搜尋兩次,而不須「上窮碧落下黃泉」。

All the good ideas I ever had came to me while I was milking a cow.

「我曾有的好點子全都是在擠牛奶的時候想出來的。」

Grant Wood 格蘭特‧伍德 (1891–1942)
美國畫家,最著名的作品為美國中西部郊區風景,《美國式歌德》 (*American Gothic*) 為二十世紀經典圖像。

伍德出生於愛荷華的農場,而且大半輩子都住在這個中西部的州內。儘管他去過歐洲多次,而且把創作委由紐約的一家畫廊代理,但是他卻是「鄉土派」的主要擁護者。該派倡導美國的鄉村主題,並力抗歐洲的藝術潮流。

👍 **Inspiration from Within** 來自內心的靈感

Do not quench your inspiration and your imagination; do not become the slave of your model.

「不要扼殺你的靈感和想像力；不要成為你的範本的奴隸。」

Vincent van Gogh 文森·梵谷 ⇨ P. 59

本句由兩個對等的否定命令句所組成。由於兩個命令句之間沒有連接詞，所以中間使用了分號。

No amount of skillful invention can replace the essential element of imagination.

「再多巧妙的發明也取代不了想像力的本質。」

Edward Hopper 愛德華·哈潑 (1882–1967)
北美最受歡迎的藝術家之一，以描繪陽光下的人群凸顯現代人寂寞單調的生活。

對於擅長於光影呈現的美國寫實派畫家哈潑而言，缺乏想像力的一幅畫，縱使畫者技巧再高超、再新穎，也是沒有什麼價值的。

Notes

quench [kwɛntʃ] *v.* 壓制；抑制

Every morning upon awakening, I experience a supreme pleasure: that of being Salvador Dali, and I ask myself, wonderstruck, what prodigious thing will he do today, this Salvador Dali.

「我每天早上醒來的時候，都覺得無比的快樂，我感受到的是身為薩爾瓦多‧達利的快感。我會非常好奇地自問，這位薩爾瓦多‧達利，他今天又要做什麼驚天動地的事。」

Salvador Dali 薩爾瓦多‧達利

除了狂妄自大之外，達利最為人所知的就是他豐富的想像力。難怪他會被超現實主義所吸引，而成為該派的超級大師。

Notes

wonderstruck [ˈwʌndəˌstrʌk] *adj.* 大吃一驚的
prodigious [prəˈdɪdʒəs] *adj.* 驚人的；奇妙的

Chapter 14

Truth and Originality

真相和原創性

Close-up

顛覆傳統的野獸派先驅

Henri Matisse

亨利‧馬蒂斯

(1869–1954)

HENRI MATISSE

Henri Matisse lived much of his life like an office worker. He woke early, put on a conservative suit, and headed to his studio to work. After a simple lunch, he would return to his studio and work some more. In the evenings he would relax by reading or playing the violin, and then go to bed early. The next day—more of the same. He said he sought "an art of balance, of purity and serenity, devoid of troubling or depressing subject matter." Not exactly the background you would expect from someone whose paintings were called "wild beasts." What Matisse managed to accomplish in his workaday way was to quietly overturn each the cornerstones that had sustained Western art for centuries. Perspective, line, and most significantly color were all repurposed for expressive ends in entirely unprecedented ways. Matisse never set out to shock, and he had no desire to offend the classical painters he loved. Matisse's originality was incidental, a byproduct of his dedication and a steadfast commitment to art itself. As a young man, he once wrote to his fiancée, "I love you dearly, mademoiselle; but I shall always love painting more." His dedication never waivered, and as an old man, he was able to write to a friend and say, finally, "I have the mastery of it [color]. I am sure of it."

亨利‧馬蒂斯的一生很多時候過得跟上班族沒兩樣。他一大早起床，穿上保守的西裝，然後到他的畫室工作。簡單用過午餐後，他會回到畫室再工作一陣子。晚上的時候，他會看看書或拉拉小提琴放鬆一下，然後早早就寢。隔天──同樣再按表操課。他說他所追尋的藝術「要均衡，純粹而平靜，完全不牽扯令人煩憂或沮喪的主題」。對於一個畫作被以「野獸」相稱的人而言，這樣的背景令人難以想像。馬蒂斯的成就在於，他把數世紀以來維繫西方藝術的基石給一一推翻。為了達到表現的目的，他將透視法、線條以及最重要的色彩徹底改觀。馬蒂斯從來無意驚世駭俗，也無意冒犯他所喜愛的古典畫家們。馬蒂斯的原創性是偶然的產物，這項副產品來自他的努力不懈，以及他對藝術本身不變的堅持。他在年輕時曾寫信給他的未婚妻說：「我愛妳至深，小姐；但是我會永遠更愛繪畫。」而他的努力從未止息，在他老的時候，他寫信跟朋友說：「我已經能完全掌握它〔色彩〕了。我很確定。」

Notes

serenity [sə`rɛnətɪ] *n.* 平靜
devoid [dɪ`vɔɪd] of 缺乏；沒有
overturn [ˌovə`tɜn] *v.* 推翻；顛覆
cornerstone [`kɔrnəˌ ston] *n.* 【建】基石
unprecedented [ʌn`prɛsəˌ dɛntɪd] *adj.*
史無前例的
byproduct [`baɪˌ prɑdəkt] *n.* 副產品
steadfast [`stɛdˌ fæst] *n.* 不變的
mastery [`mæstərɪ] *n.* 精通；掌握

> *There is nothing more difficult for a truly creative painter than to paint a rose, because before he can do so he has first to forget all the roses that were ever painted.*

Henri Matisse

「對一個眞正有創意的畫家而言，最難的事莫過於畫玫瑰，因爲他必須先把以往所畫過的玫瑰全部忘掉，才能畫得出來。」

英文用法解析

我們可以把馬蒂斯的這句話跟達利說過的："The first man to compare the cheeks of a young woman to a rose was obviously a poet; the first to repeat it was possibly an idiot."「第一個把年輕女子的雙頰比喻為玫瑰的人顯然是個詩人；第一個把它重述一遍的人則可能是個白癡。」這句話拿來做個比較。

藝術有賴（世界之）重現與（藝術家之）表現的怪異結合，這種在複製與原創性之間所產生的緊張關係就是藝術之基礎。野獸派大師馬蒂斯的正直或許是天生的，而他的原創性或許是從事這個行業的自然結果，但是，就跟各個時代的各個流派的藝術家一樣，對於真相、模仿和原創性等問題，他是經過深思熟慮的。從本章中各式各樣（有時互相矛盾）的觀點中可以看出，我們沒有理由相信這種緊張關係會有消弭的一天。

Truth and Originality 2

" Exactitude is not truth.

「精準並不等於真相。」

Henri Matisse　亨利・馬蒂斯

馬蒂斯最引發爭議的畫作之一就是《戴帽子的女人》(*Woman with a Hat*)。該幅畫畫的是馬蒂斯的妻子，他在畫中使用的盡是不該出現在某些地方的鮮豔色彩：額頭是綠的、下巴是紫的、鼻頭是黃的。這些顏色和其他更多的色彩則在她的衣服上反覆出現。在被問到妻子當時究竟是穿什麼顏色的衣服時，他開玩笑說：「當然是黑色的。」

Truth and Originality 3

" Writing graffiti is about the most honest way you can be an artist. It takes no money to do it, you don't need an education to understand it and there's no admission fee.

「街頭塗鴉可以說是成為藝術家最直率的方式。你不必花錢就能做，不用人教就看得懂，而且不收門票。」

Banksy　班斯基

班斯基還說過："Become good at cheating and you never need to become good at anything."「只要你很會說謊，其他任何事你就都不須要會了。」

I prefer drawing to talking. Drawing is faster, and leaves less room for lies.

「我喜歡畫畫，而不喜歡說話。畫畫比較快，說謊的空間也比較小。」

Le Corbusier 柯比意 (1887–1965)
瑞士建築師與藝術家，透過不斷繪畫與建築的實驗，成為現代建築的先鋒。

Prefer A to B 是常用的片語，意思是「較喜歡 A，而較不喜歡 B」。記得 A、B 兩項（通常是名詞或動名詞）必須對等。

All works of art created by truthful minds without regard for the work's conventional exterior remain genuine for all times.

「不管作品的傳統外貌為何，真誠心靈所創作出來的一切藝術作品都會歷久彌堅。」

Franz Marc 法蘭茲・馬克

從修辭的角度來看這個句子並不理想，因為主詞 All works of art ... exterior 顯然過長，讓人有頭重腳輕之覺。若將介系詞片語 without regard for ... exterior 由主詞部分脫離，移至句首，整句話會較容易理解：Without ... exterior, all works of art created by truthful minds remain genuine for all time.。

Notes

exactitude [ɪɡˋzæktə͵tjud] *n.* 正確

We all know that Art is not truth. Art is a lie that makes us realize the truth, at least the truth that is given to us to understand.

「大家都知道，藝術並非真相。藝術是使我們明白真相的謊言，至少是我們有機會了解的真相。」

Pablo Picasso 帕布羅·畢卡索 ⇨P. 1

依照畢卡索的邏輯，「藝術」顯然是一種「必要之惡」(necessary evil)，除非我門無意知道真相為何。

Truth exists; only lies are invented.

「真相是存在的；只有謊言才要捏造。」

Georges Braque 喬治·布拉克 (1882–1963)

法國畫家與雕刻家，歷經後印象派、野獸派，最後與畢卡索共創立體派。

的確，真相就是真相，唯有不希望真相被發掘的人才會說謊，製造「假」相。

What is truth? Truth doesn't really exist. Who is going to judge whether my experience of an incident is more valid than yours? No one can be trusted to be the judge of that.

「真相是什麼？真相其實並不存在。誰能評斷說，我對於一個事件的體驗是否比你真確？在這件事的評斷上，沒有人可以被信賴。」

Tracey Emin 翠西・艾敏 (1963–)
英國當代藝術家，為英國青年藝術家成員之一。

艾敏和布拉克的看法完全相反：布拉克認為真相存在，艾敏卻不以為然。誰是誰非？根結應該在於兩人對「真相」的認知有所差異。

Notes

valid [ˈvælɪd] *adj.* （議論、理由等）有確實根據的；正確的

👍 Copying 模仿

Those who do not want to imitate anything, produce nothing.

「什麼都不想模仿的人，什麼都做不出來。」

Salvador Dali 薩爾瓦多‧達利

的確，除了上帝之外（如果你相信有上帝），人是無法 create anything out of nothing 的。在藝術的領域裡「複製」、「模仿」並非罪惡（我們可以想像貝多芬的「田園交響曲」已經被「複製」過多少次），重點在於複製者能展面什麼樣的原創性。

Bad artists copy. Good artists steal.

「差勁的藝術家靠模仿。優秀的藝術家靠竊取。」

Pablo Picasso 帕布羅‧畢卡索

畢卡索肯定師法他人的重要性，但是卻厭惡自我重複。他曾經說："To copy others is necessary, but to copy oneself is pathetic." 「模仿別人有其必要，但是模仿自己就很可悲了。」

The painter who draws merely by practice and by eye, without any reason, is like a mirror which copies everything placed in front of it without being conscious of their existence.

「要是畫家只靠練習和眼睛來作畫，而沒有任何理由，就會像是一面鏡子，只能複製放在它前面的每樣東西，卻無法意識到這些東西的存在。」

Leonardo da Vinci 李奧納多‧達文西

達文西的技藝在史上鮮少有人能與其相提並論，但是連他都認為，完美的技巧永遠是達到目的的手段，而不是目的本身。

I had to create an equivalent for what I felt about what I was looking at—not copy it.

「我必須創造出一件能完全呈現我對於所見事物之感受的作品，而不是複製它。」

Georgia O'Keeffe 喬琪亞‧歐姬芙

換句話說，歐姬芙的作品呈現的是她對所見事物所做的詮釋，而非像鏡子裡頭的影像，只反映出事物的表面。這個看法和達文西的見解相近。

Truth and Originality 13

Students worry too much about originality. The emphasis on original, individual work in the past years has done a great deal to produce a crop of eccentric fakes and has carried art away from the stream of tradition. Tradition is our heritage of knowledge and experience. We can't get along without it.

「研究藝術的人對原創性擔心過了頭。過去幾年對於原創、獨特作品過度強調的結果，造就了一堆奇奇怪怪的假貨，並使得藝術偏離了傳統的潮流。傳統是我們的知識與經驗的遺產，少了它我們就無以為繼。」

John Sloan 約翰・史隆

第一句話的 student 除用來指「學生」外，也可用來指專門研究某領域的「學者」。第二句的 a crop of 指「一群、大量的……」，而 fake 在此作名詞用，意思是「冒牌貨、仿造品」。末尾句中的 get along 可用來指「過活」、「(和睦)相處」，在此較接近第一個意思。

Truth and Originality 14

Do not worry about your originality. You could not get rid of it even if you wanted to.

「別擔心你的原創性。你就算想甩掉它你也甩不掉。」

Robert Henri 羅勃・亨利

這句話令亨利的許多學生，包括愛德華・哈潑 (Edward Hopper)、喬治・貝羅斯 (George Bellows)，以及約瑟夫・史特拉 (Joseph Stella)，寬心不少。

Imitation is not inspiration, and inspiration only can give birth to a work of art. The least of man's original emanation is better than the best of borrowed thought.

「模仿並不是靈感，而靈感只會創作出藝術作品。人最渺小的原創火花也比最優秀的拾人牙慧要強。」

Albert Pinkham Ryder 亞伯特・平克姆・萊德 (1847–1917)
美國畫家，賦予寓言畫如詩般變化莫測的氛圍和海景。

Give birth to 原意為「生（孩子）」，在此指的是「創作出（藝術品）」。另，emanation 原指「放射（物）」、「發散（物）」，在此則用來表達原創力的迸發。

N o t e s

heritage [ˈhɛrətɪdʒ] *n.* 遺產
fake [fek] *n.* 仿造品；贗品
emanation [ɛməˈneʃən] *n.* 放射；發散

In art, all who have done something other than their predecessors have merited the epithet of revolutionary; and it is they alone who are masters.

「在藝術中，只要能做到有別於前人的事全都應該被封為革命家；只有他們才是大師。」

Paul Gauguin 保羅‧高更 ⇨P. 147

本句中的 merit 為動詞用法，意思是「應得、應受」。

Notes

predecessor [ˈprɛdɪˌsɛsə] *n.* 前輩
epithet [ˈɛpɪθɛt] *n.*（描述性）稱號
revolutionary [ˌrɛvəˈluʃənˌɛrɪ] *n.* 革命者

Chapter 15

Work
工作

Close-up

無可取代的曠世全才
Leonardo da Vinci
達文西 (1452–1519)

LEONARDO DA VINCI

In 1481, Leonardo da Vinci applied for a job with the future Duke of Milan. His cover letter is a classic. Her runs through a long list of his engineering and military talents—the man knows how to construct bridges, attack walled cities, dig tunnels, build ships, tanks, and missiles—and finishes up by almost offhandedly noting that he can paint pretty well too. One does wonder how he had time to design his airplanes and submarines while at the same time conducting wide-ranging studies anatomy, geography, astronomy, and numerous other fields. (He also squeezed in time to knock out the *Mona Lisa*.) The truth is Leonardo was a bit of procrastinator: he designed more than he built, and he sketched more than he painted. He spent years working on *The Last Supper*, sometimes working around the clock, other times going days without lifting a brush. Leonardo's attitude toward work is perhaps best appreciated through a joke, perhaps funny by Renaissance standards, that he included in one of his notebooks: "A man was desired to rise from bed, because the sun was already risen. To which he replied: 'If I had as far to go, and as much to do as he has, I should be risen by now; but having but a little way to go, I shall not rise yet'."

1481 年時,達文西去應徵工作,對象是未來的米蘭公爵。他的求職信很經典。他羅列了一長串本身的工程與軍事長才——顯示出他這個人懂得怎麼造橋、攻城池、挖隧道,也知道如何建造船艦、坦克和飛彈——只在結尾時一語帶過說他對於繪畫也十分在行。令人深感納悶的是,他怎麼有時間在設計飛機和潛艇的同時,又能廣泛地研究解剖學、地理學、天文學,以及其他許許多多的學門,還擠出時間完成了《蒙娜麗莎》。其實達文西有點愛拖:他設計的東西比實際做出來的多,打的草稿比真正完成的畫多。他畫《最後的晚餐》就花了好幾年的時間,有時他會日以繼夜地畫,有時則是一停筆就好幾天。從一則笑話中或許最能看出達文西對工作的態度——以文藝復興時期的標準來看,這則笑話應該是滿好笑的。他在一本筆記簿裡寫道:「有個人被要求起床,因為太陽已經出來了。對此他回應說:『假如我跟他一樣有那麼遠的路要走,有那麼多事要做,那我現在真該起來。可是我只有一小段路要走,所以我還不打算起來。』」

Notes

missile [ˋmɪsl] *n.* 飛彈
offhandedly [ɔfˋhændɪdlɪ] *adv.* 隨便地;漫不經心地
anatomy [əˋnætəmɪ] *n.* 解剖學
astronomy [əˋstrɑnəmɪ] *n.* 天文學
procrastinator [proˋkræstə͵netə] *n.* 拖延之人
around the clock 日以繼夜地

"As a well-spent day brings happy sleep, so a life well spent brings happy death.

Leonardo da Vinci

「正如充實地過一天可換來愉快的睡眠，充實地過一生可換來愉快的死亡。」

英文用法解析

達文西在這句話中利用 As ..., so .... 的句型做了一個有趣的類比。的確，要睡好覺、要得好死，日子就要過得充實。

談到工作，藝術家其實跟一般人沒什麼兩樣。有的人（比如像莫里斯、畢卡索、馬丁和葛里斯）力求聰明工作。他們認為，工作應該要有尊嚴、有意義、有樂趣。而就跟大多數人一樣，大部分藝術家工作都很努力。從文藝復興時代的米開朗基羅到 20 世紀的亨利‧摩爾 (Henry Moore) 都認為，努力工作不僅是成功的手段，而且是一種美德。當然，也有別的藝術家對於工作的必要性抱持著比較負面的看法。像沃荷、班斯基、惠斯勒、羅斯金等眼光獨到的文化評論家便指出，要是工作的條件或目的令人不快，那就連做都不該做。

Work 2

Nothing should be made by man's labour which is not worth making; or which must be made by labour degrading to the makers.

「人不該付出勞力去做任何一件不值得做，或是必須靠有辱工作者人格之勞力才能完成的事。」

William Morris　威廉·莫里斯

少有藝術家像威廉·莫里斯這麼關切工作的本質。除了是藝術與工藝運動的領袖之外（他提倡以傳統手工藝來因應十九世紀沒有靈魂的工業化），莫里斯在英國早期的社會主義中也扮演了重要的角色。

Work 3

Never permit a dichotomy to rule your life, a dichotomy in which you hate what you do so you can have pleasure in your spare time. Look for a situation in which your work will give you as much happiness as your spare time.

「千萬不要讓二分法支配你的生活，一種因為你討厭你做的工作，所以只有在閒暇時才能夠獲得樂趣的二分法。找出一個工作時能帶給你跟閒暇時一樣多快樂的狀況。」

Dichotomy 這個字源自希臘文，dicho 指 "in two"，tomy 指 "cut"，意即「一切為二」。畢卡索的意思簡單說就是：我們應該做我們喜歡的工作，並樂在其中。

Work 4

> *To progress in life you must give up the things you do not like. Give up doing the things that you do not like to do. You must find the things that you do like. The things that are acceptable to your mind.*

「生活如果要有進展，你就必須放棄你不喜歡的東西，要放棄做你不喜歡做的事。必須找出你真正喜歡的東西，你心裡所能接受的東西。」

Agnes Martin 艾妮絲 · 馬丁 (1912–2004)
美國現代藝術家，作品以東方哲學思維、線條與格子呈現極限主義風格。

需特別留意的是，第三句中的 do 為助動詞，在此處是為了用來強調其後的動詞 like。

N o t e s

degrade [dɪˋgred] *v.* 降低……的地位
dichotomy [daɪˋkɑtəmɪ] *n.* 二分法

I always pet a dog with my left hand because if he bit me I'd still have my right hand to paint with.

「我一向用左手逗狗，因為萬一他咬我，我還能用右手來畫畫。」

Juan Gris 胡安‧葛里斯

本句中的 pet 為動詞，意思是「撫弄」，pet a dog 就是「逗狗」。由這句話可以看出葛里斯對工作的態度。葛理斯為立體派大師，1912 年時曾為畢卡索畫了一幅立體式肖像畫。連畢卡索本人都對他的畫作讚嘆不已。

👍 **Work Hard** 努力工作

If you knew how much work went into it, you would not call it genius.

「假如你知道那有多費工，你就不會說那是天才了。」

Michelangelo 米開朗基羅

米開朗基羅在此所說的是他在西斯廷教堂所作的畫。這項工作讓他過了難熬的四年——在那片屋頂上作畫可說是費盡千辛萬苦。我們應該這麼說，西斯廷教堂的屋頂就跟大部分的傑作一樣，是天才加上努力的結果。

Work 7

Work cures everything.

「工作可以治療一切。」

Henri Matisse　亨利・馬蒂斯 ⇨P. 191

野獸派大師馬蒂斯只用三個字道出他對工作的看法。這句話與我們常聽到的 "Time cures everything."「時間可以治療一切。」相當不一樣。馬蒂斯的話充滿了正面、積極的意義。

Work 8

One must work and dare if one really wants to live.

「假如人真的想活下去，他就必須工作，並且有膽量。」

Vincent van Gogh　文森・梵谷 ⇨P. 59

與馬蒂斯相同，梵谷對於工作一樣抱持極為正面的態度。相信也是因為這種強烈的信念讓梵谷能在痛苦的環境下持續創作。

Work 9

> *Do all the work you can; that is the whole philosophy of the good way of life.*

「做好你能做的所有工作；這就是生活良方的全部哲學。」

Eugene Delacroix　尤金・德拉克洛瓦

法國浪漫派畫家德拉克洛瓦說的這句話似乎並不「浪漫」。我們可以很確定的是，一個工作不努力的人是沒有資格談浪漫的。

Work 10

> *I know of no genius but the genius of hard work.*

「除了努力工作的天才之外，我不知道有什麼天才。」

J. M. W. Turner　J. M. W. 泰納 (1775–1851)
英國浪漫主義風景畫家，以色彩變化技法將風景畫的地位提升至與歷史畫抗衡。

泰納的這句話與愛迪生 (Thomas Edison) 所說的："Genius is one percent inspiration, ninety-nine percent perspiration." 「天才是百分之一的靈感加上百分之九十九的汗水。」有異曲同工之妙。

If you have great talents, industry will improve them: if you have but moderate abilities, industry will supply their deficiency.

「如果你有天分，勤奮可以強化它：如果你只有中等的能力，勤奮則能補其不足。」

Joshua Reynolds 　約書亞·雷諾茲

Industry 源自拉丁文，原意即為「勤奮」，一般作「工業；產業」解乃後來引申之意義。由於字義用法之不同，也必須注意衍生出的不同形容詞：industrious 指「勤奮的」；industrial 則指「工業的；產業的」。

Work 12

No masterpiece was ever created by a lazy artist.

「從來沒有一幅傑作是由懶惰的藝術家所創作出來的。」

Salvador Dali 　薩爾瓦多·達利

依照達利的邏輯，他肯定是一個 industrious「勤奮的」藝術家，因為他創作出一幅幅的 masterpieces。

Notes

moderate [ˋmɑdərɪt] *adj.* 中等的
deficiency [dɪˋfɪʃənsɪ] *n.* 不足

There's no retirement for an artist, it's your way of living so there's no end to it.

「藝術家是不退休的，那是你的生活方式，所以沒有終點。」

Henry Moore 亨利·摩爾 (1898–1986)
英國雕塑家，以銅或大理石為媒材，雕塑出圓滑、抽象造形的人體。

就口說而言，這句話「聽」起來並沒有什麼問題，但是用文字來表達時卻可發現這個句子似乎少了一個連接詞（一共有三個子句，卻只有一個連接詞so）。如前面提及的，一個補救的方式就是把句中的逗號改為分號，如此一來既不會影響原句的節奏韻律，在文法修辭上也就無懈可擊了。

👍 **Work Less** 減少工作

Work 14

I suppose I have a really loose interpretation of "work" because I think that just being alive is so much work at something you don't always want to do. Being born is like being kidnapped. And then sold into slavery. People are working every minute. The machinery is always going. Even when you sleep.

「我想我對於『工作』的詮釋相當寬鬆，因為我認為光是活著就意味著你得做一大堆你並非一直想做的事。出生有如遭到了綁架，然後又被賣去當奴隸。人每分鐘都在工作，機器一直在運轉，就連你在睡覺的時候也一樣。」

Andy Warhol　安迪‧沃荷

相信有很多人都覺得「活得很累」，但是相信也有很多人願意和安迪‧沃荷交換位子，享受他所獲得的肯定與榮耀。

Work 15

The artist's only positive virtue is idleness—and there are so few who are gifted at it.

「藝術家唯一正面的美德就是賦閒——而有這種天賦的人少之又少。」

James Whistler　詹姆斯‧惠斯勒

Idle「賦閒」就是什麼事都不幹。的確，也只有像惠斯勒這種大師級的藝術家（他是倡導 art for art's sake「為藝術而藝術」的指標型人物）才有資格享受這樣的 luxury「好康」。

Notes

kidnap [ˋkɪdnæp] *v.* 綁架、誘拐（小孩）
gifted [ˋgɪftɪd] *adj.* （在……方面）有天才的

People who get up early in the morning cause war, death and famine.

「在晨間早起的人會導致戰爭、死亡和饑荒。」

Banksy 班斯基

「非法」塗鴉的藝術特性使班斯基必須在夜間工作,但是我們不該因此而忽略他這句話的重點:本質上工作不見得是件好事。每天都在進行的工作,有很多不做反而比較好。

No small misery is caused by overworked and unhappy people, in the dark views which they necessarily take up themselves, and force upon others, of work itself.

「工作過度和不快樂的人會造成不小的悲劇,這些人自己必然是對工作本身產生了負面的看法,並強加諸於他人身上。」

John Ruskin 約翰‧羅斯金

No small misery 「不小的悲劇」就是「大的悲劇」。依照羅斯金的看法,如果工作不愉快那就乾脆不要做,免得牽拖到別人。

Notes

famine [ˈfæmɪn] *n.* 飢荒

Get a Feel for English!

向125位菁英看齊， 從閱讀頂尖領袖經典名言開始！

定價：220元（1書+1MP3）

一句話許你
一個觀點，一個夢想，
一份改變的勇氣，一股前進的力量

★ 名言雋語，培養英文閱讀與寫作正確途徑
★ 多益、托福、雅思、大學考試強化實力必讀
★ 中英對照＋用語解析，同步深化人生智慧＆英文實力

貝塔語言出版
Beta Multimedia Publishing

隨查即用超方便，
貝塔ＡＰＰ電子書

精選高頻必備語句及字彙，
臨場反應輕鬆面對！

商務溝通

檢定考試

生活應用

立即購買 $2.99 USD

必通語句列表 主題情境對話，外師親聲朗讀

關鍵字查詢 查閱相關語句內容

學習記錄 檢視學習成效

急救箱 方便特定場合快速查閱

測驗 檢視學習成果

貝塔行動電子書櫃

國家圖書館出版品預行編目資料

最有力量的英文－藝術天才經典名言／David Katz, 王復國作：
 戴至中譯. -- 初版. -- 臺北市：貝塔出版：智勝文化發行, 2011.09
  面： 公分

 ISBN: 978-957-729-851-5（平裝）

 1. 英語 2. 讀本 3. 格言

805.18   100012664

最有力量的英文－藝術天才經典名言

作　　者／David Katz、王復國
譯　　者／戴至中
執行編輯／莊碧娟
文字整理／杜文田

出　　版／貝塔出版有限公司
地　　址／100 台北市館前路 12 號 11 樓
郵　　撥／19493777 貝塔出版有限公司
客服專線／(02) 2314-3535　傳　　真／(02) 2312-3535
客服信箱／btservice@betamedia.com.tw

總 經 銷／時報文化出版企業股份有限公司
地　　址／桃園縣龜山鄉萬壽路二段 351 號
電　　話／(02) 2306-6842

出版日期／2011 年 9 月初版一刷
定　　價／250 元
I S B N／978-957-729-851-5

Copyright 2011 by Beta Multimedia Publishing Co., Ltd.

貝塔網址：www.betamedia.com.tw
本書之文字、圖形、設計均係著作權所有，若有抄襲、模仿、冒用等情事，
依法追究。如有缺頁、破損、裝訂錯誤，請寄回本公司調換

喚醒你的英文語感！

折後釘好，直接寄回即可！

| 廣 告 回 信 |
| 北區郵政管理局登記證 |
| 北 台 字 第 1 4 2 5 6 號 |
| 免 貼 郵 票 |

100 台北市中正區館前路12號11樓

 貝塔語言出版 收
Beta Multimedia Publishing

寄件者住址 ☐☐☐

貝塔語言出版
Beta Multimedia Publishing

讀者服務專線（02）2314-3535　　讀者服務傳真（02）2312-35

客戶服務信箱 btservice@betamedia.com.tw

www.betamedia.com.tw

謝謝您購買本書！！

貝塔語言擁有最優良之英文學習書籍，為提供您最佳的英語學習資訊，您可填妥此表後寄回（免貼郵票）將可不定期收到本公司最新發行書訊及活動訊息！

姓名：_____　性別：□男 □女　生日：____年____月____日

電話：(公)_____(宅)_____(手機)_____

電子信箱：_____

學歷：□高中職含以下 □專科 □大學 □研究所含以上

職業：□金融 □服務 □傳播 □製造 □資訊 □軍公教 □出版

　　　□自由 □教育 □學生 □其他

職級：□企業負責人 □高階主管 □中階主管 □職員 □專業人士

1. 您購買的書籍是？_____

2. 您從何處得知本產品？(可複選)

　　　□書店 □網路 □書展 □校園活動 □廣告信函 □他人推薦 □新聞報導 □其他

3. 您覺得本產品價格：

　　　□偏高 □合理 □偏低

4. 請問目前您每週花了多少時間學英語？

　　　□ 不到十分鐘 □ 十分鐘以上，但不到半小時 □ 半小時以上，但不到一小時

　　　□ 一小時以上，但不到兩小時 □ 兩個小時以上 □ 不一定

5. 通常在選擇語言學習書時，哪些因素是您會考慮的？

　　　□ 封面 □ 內容、實用性 □ 品牌 □ 媒體、朋友推薦 □ 價格 □ 其他_____

6. 市面上您最需要的語言書種類為？

　　　□ 聽力 □ 閱讀 □ 文法 □ 口說 □ 寫作 □ 其他_____

7. 通常您會透過何種方式選購語言學習書籍？

　　　□ 書店門市 □ 網路書店 □ 郵購 □ 直接找出版社 □ 學校或公司團購

　　　□ 其他_____

8. 給我們的建議：_____

_____

喚醒你的英文語感 ！

Get a Feel for English !